The Mirror Realm

(The Lacey Swift Series)
Book One

Tim O'Rourke

First Edition Published by Ravenwoodgreys

Copyright 2017 by Tim O'Rourke

Story Editor
Lynda O'Rourke
Book cover designed by:
Orina Kafe
www.facebook.com/OrinaKafeArtworks
Copyedited by:
Carolyn M. Pinard

For Joseph, Thomas & Zachary

More books by Tim O'Rourke

Kiera Hudson Series One
Vampire Shift (Kiera Hudson Series 1) Book 1
Vampire Wake (Kiera Hudson Series 1) Book 2
Vampire Hunt (Kiera Hudson Series 1) Book 3
Vampire Breed (Kiera Hudson Series 1) Book 4
Wolf House (Kiera Hudson Series 1) Book 5
Vampire Hollows (Kiera Hudson Series 1) Book 6
Kiera Hudson Series Two
Dead Flesh (Kiera Hudson Series 2) Book 1
Dead Night (Kiera Hudson Series 2) Book 2
Dead Angels (Kiera Hudson Series 2) Book 3
Dead Statues (Kiera Hudson Series 2) Book 4
Dead Seth (Kiera Hudson Series 2) Book 5
Dead Wolf (Kiera Hudson Series 2) Book 6
Dead Water (Kiera Hudson Series 2) Book 7
Dead Push (Kiera Hudson Series 2) Book 8
Dead Lost (Kiera Hudson Series 2) Book 9
Dead End (Kiera Hudson Series 2) Book 10
Kiera Hudson Series Three
The Creeping Men (Kiera Hudson Series Three)
Book 1
The Lethal Infected (Kiera Hudson Series Three)
Book 2
The Adoring Artist (Kiera Hudson Series Three)
Book 3
The Secret Identity (Kiera Hudson Series Three)
Book 4

The White Wolf (Kiera Hudson Series Three)
Book 5
The Origins of Cara (Kiera Hudson Series Three)
Book 6
The Final Push (Kiera Hudson Series Three)
Book 7
The Underground Switch (Kiera Hudson Series Three) Book 8

The Kiera Hudson Prequels

The Kiera Hudson Prequels (Book One)
The Kiera Hudson Prequels (Book Two)

Kiera Hudson & Sammy Carter

Vampire Twin (*Pushed* Trilogy) Book 1
Vampire Chronicle (*Pushed* Trilogy) Book 2

The Alternate World of Kiera Hudson

Wolf Shift

Werewolves of Shade

Werewolves of Shade (Part One)
Werewolves of Shade (Part Two)
Werewolves of Shade (Part Three)
Werewolves of Shade (Part Four)
Werewolves of Shade (Part Five)
Werewolves of Shade (Part Six)

Vampires of Maze

Vampires of Maze (Part One)
Vampires of Maze (Part Two)
Vampires of Maze (Part Three)
Vampires of Maze (Part Four)
Vampires of Maze (Part Five)

Vampires of Maze (Part Six)
Witches of Twisted Den
Witches of Twisted Den (Part One)
Witches of Twisted Den (Part Two)
Witches of Twisted Den (Part Three)
Witches of Twisted Den (Part Four)
Witches of Twisted Den (Part Five)
Witches of Twisted Den (Part Six)
Cowgirl & Creature (Laura Pepper Series)
Cowgirl & Creature (Part One)
Cowgirl & Creature (Part Two)
Cowgirl & Creature (Part Three)
Cowgirl & Creature (Part Four)
Cowgirl & Creature (Part Five)
Cowgirl & Creature (Part Six)
Cowgirl & Creature (Part Seven)
Cowgirl & Creature (Part Eight)
The Mirror Realm
The Mirror Realm (Book One)
Moon Trilogy
Moonlight (Moon Trilogy) Book 1
Moonbeam (Moon Trilogy) Book 2
Moonshine (Moon Trilogy) Book 3
The Jack Seth Novellas
Hollow Pit (Book One)
Black Hill Farm (Books 1 & 2)
Black Hill Farm (Book 1)
Black Hill Farm: Andy's Diary (Book 2)
Sidney Hart Novels

Witch (A Sidney Hart Novel) Book 1
Yellow (A Sidney Hart Novel) Book 2
The Tessa Dark Trilogy
Stilts (Book 1)
Zip (Book 2)
The Mechanic
The Mechanic
The Dark Side of Nightfall Trilogy
The Dark Side of Nightfall (Book One)
The Dark Side of Nightfall (Book Two)
The Dark Side of Nightfall (Book Three)
Samantha Carter Series
Vampire Seeker (Book One)
Vampire Flappers (Book Two)
Vampire Watchmen (Book Three)
Unscathed
Written by Tim O'Rourke & C.J. Pinard
You can contact Tim O'Rourke at
www.facebook.com/timorourkeauthor/ or by
email at kierahudson91@aol.com

The Mirror Realm

(Book One)

Chapter One

Lacey Swift raced through the snow, ignoring the giant flakes that swirled all about her. Plumes of breath jetted from her mouth and nose, her long, blonde hair stuck to the sides of her face. She pulled the hood of her sweatshirt over her head in an attempt to stay warm. Lacey glanced back over her shoulder for any sign of the man who would soon come in search of her once he realised she had escaped from the house where she and her twin sister had been kept prisoners by him. It had taken her some years to learn her uncle wasn't trying to help neither her nor her sister, Thea, but was poisoning them. But as her nineteenth birthday had approached, Lacey had learnt how to fool her uncle into believing she was swallowing the pills he gave her daily, when really she was holding them in the back of her throat, ready to spit them out once he had left her room.

Fearing that her uncle might have already discovered that he had been deceived by her, Lacey ran faster and further with every stride, even though her lungs were screaming for her to stop. But Lacey didn't listen nor care. She had suddenly tasted freedom and she devoured it.

She wouldn't stop running until she had found her way out of the woods, reached the nearest town, and managed to raise the alarm. Nothing would stop her or get in her way until she had brought help to save Thea, who still lay unconscious and close to death in the upstairs room at her uncle's cottage.

Ahead of her, the snowflakes continued to swirl and collide with each other like a shifting white wall. The leafless trees stood thin and black against the sky. Her trainers pounded over and through the snow, sending up white puffs with every stride she took. Beginning to feel close to exhaustion, Lacey glanced back again in search of her uncle. But the snowfall was so thick, it was impossible to see much further than a few feet behind her. She gasped in lungfuls of freezing cold air and listened for any sound. There was none. No sound of footsteps in the snow behind her. Facing front again, Lacey trudged on, each stride more sluggish now as the cold wind bit at her, sapping her strength. But she wouldn't let it drain her resolve. She had waited to make her escape for months and wouldn't be defeated now that she was free. Each pill she had spat out when her uncle's back had been turned had been a challenge – a challenge that had, with each passing day, become more exciting and exhilarating. Those feelings reminded her that danger could be conquered, and so too could her uncle.

Fearing that she would never find her way out of the woods that stretched away from behind her uncle's remote cottage, Lacey slowed. She looked left and right, wondering if perhaps she had not been simply running in a wide circle. It seemed like a very long time ago that she had left the cottage and ventured into the woods or anywhere else. Lacey hadn't attended college in a very long time, because she had fallen ill and her uncle had started treating her with his noxious medicine. She'd had friends at college, but they had stopped calling some time ago – her uncle had made sure of that. And now that she had managed to set herself free – now that she had ventured into the woods once more – every part of it looked the same. She could not see one distinguishing feature. Everything looked white. The wind moaned, buffeting against her. She wobbled on her feet as if the biting wind was testing her – trying to knock her over. Did it sense weakness? But she wasn't weak. She had spent much of the last few years feeling weak. But not anymore. Over the last few months she had grown strong. She believed that. Lacey had to, if she was to keep going – to keep running. There was no way she would let her uncle catch her. Lacey would not allow herself to be taken back to that house. She was no longer a little girl. She had recently turned nineteen – become a young woman – a young woman who refused to remain a prisoner. She and her twin sister had been nothing more than their uncle's prisoners since their parents' deaths some years before. Grief tightened Lacey's throat as she remembered her parents. She pushed them from her mind, fearing that her heartache might slow her down.

Lacey pushed on, hands and face now feeling numb with cold. The snow began to harden, no longer featherlike. It jabbed at her face and the backs of her hands like needlepoints. And despite her near exhaustion and the numbing cold, Lacey smiled to herself. She was free. Lacey sensed victory was close. But she wouldn't salute herself until Thea was free too. Oxygen raced into her mouth as she sucked air into her lungs. Lacey had never run so hard, or so fast. She had been too weak before. But she was getting stronger.

Wiping the driving snow from her eyes, Lacey looked up. Rolling snowdrifts leant against the trees, and the world almost seemed to spin all around her, like she had escaped from her uncle only to find herself ensnared in a giant snow-globe that had been fiercely shaken. Yet, as Lacey peered through the churning snow, she thought she could see something else. Something new. Something strange. Slowing to a complete stop and tucking her hands into her jeans pockets, shielding them against the cold, Lacey stood staring at the figure who had appeared between the trees just ahead. This person had materialised so suddenly that at first she feared it was her uncle. But within an instant, she could see that it wasn't. The figure was too short. Too thin, and wore clothes that her uncle wouldn't be seen dead in. The clothing was identical to Lacey's. The hooded sweater was the same shade of grey, jeans the same faded blue, trainers black and covered in snow. Very slowly, Lacey took a step forward, and so did the stranger just ahead of her. Lacey stopped and so did the other. She peered out from beneath her hood and the stranger mimicked her. She raised her hand to her mouth and gasped. The person peering from beneath the hood was her identical twin. Thea had somehow managed to escape from their uncle too.

Desperate to be held by her sister, Lacey shot forward through the snow. "Thea, you've escaped!"

The other cried the same as she, too, came running forward, arms open.

But why is my sister calling me Thea? Lacey wondered as she ran to meet her sister. As she reached for Thea's hand, her fingers brushed against glass. Against a mirror. A mirror that was protruding from the snow.

Chapter Two

The wind blew a gust of snow into her face and against the glass protrusion. A curtain of hair flapped in front of her eyes, which she knocked away with one hand. Her sister did the very same thing on the other side of the mirror. Lacey pulled back her hood, anxious to get a better look. But every movement Lacey made, however subtle, her sister mimicked in every way.

"Thea, is that you?" Lacey whispered over the groan of the wind. The reflection uttered the exact same words at the very same moment as Lacey had. Frowning, she began to wonder if she wasn't staring at her identical twin sister, but simply her own reflection. But why would there be a long, tall mirror sticking out of the snow in the middle of the woods? She ran her gaze up and down the mirror and the girl on the other side of the mirror did the same. The mirror didn't appear to be attached to anything. There wasn't a frame and nothing visible that was keeping it upright or in place.

Lacey glanced over her shoulder, looking back through the woods. The only thing she could see was her own trail of footprints, now being covered by the falling snow. Apart from her, the wood appeared to be desolate, and she wasn't surprised. Who else would be mad enough to be out in the wind and snow on a freezing cold December afternoon? Lacey knew she had good reason to be out in the woods, despite the freezing weather, so who then had set the mirror in place? And why would anyone do such a bizarre thing?

The wind's icy fingers clawed at Lacey's face and she turned away to gaze back at the mirror. She frowned again, and so did her reflection. However mad the idea seemed, Lacey still clung to some hope that the girl on the other side of the mirror was truly Thea. Lacey desperately wanted to believe that her sister had escaped their uncle, too. As Lacey stood in the swirling snow and looked at the young woman in the mirror, she knew that she was identical to Thea in every way – except the scar. The scar that ran across the back of Lacey's wrist was jagged and mauve. It had been there for as long as she could remember, but couldn't recall the injury that had caused it. Ever since she had been very small, it had been there. It had never grown smaller or fainter. She had often wondered if it was not, in fact, a birthmark. But it was too thin and jagged to have been such a thing. It looked too much like it had once been a deep cut. Lacey had once asked her parents how she had come by such a scar, but neither of them had been able to recall what incident had marked her. Lacey could remember her mother saying that children often fell down and hurt themselves and she couldn't be expected to remember each one. But Lacey felt sure that her mother would have remembered such an incident because the size and colour of the scar suggested that the cut, which had caused it, would have been deep and would have needed to be stitched.

So rolling up the sleeve of her sweater, Lacey revealed the scar. She raised her arm before the mirror and couldn't help but feel her heart sting when she saw the girl in the mirror had an identical mark about her wrist. Pulling down her sleeve, Lacey knew that, without doubt, she had been looking at nothing more that her own reflection.

So why was there a mirror in the middle of the woods? Curiosity pushed Lacey toward it. She peered around the edge of the mirror to see what lay behind. She wasn't too surprised to find more snow, trees, fallen leaves, and branches covering the ground.

"Who would leave a mirror standing in the middle of the woods?" she whispered to herself, studying the mirror from each side and angle.

Lacey stepped closer still and traced circles over the smooth surface with her fingertips. A surge of energy suddenly leapt from the glass, causing her arm to prickle with pins and needles.

She snapped her hand away and rubbed the scar that circled her wrist. It suddenly throbbed with pain. "That hurt!"

Lacey continued to rub her wrist, and as she did so, she couldn't take her eyes off the mirror and her own reflection. The urge to reach out and touch the glass was too much to resist. Lacey stretched out her hand once more, placing it flat against the mirror. That surge of energy raced up her arm then exploded across her chest, knocking her backwards into the snow. Dazed and disorientated, Lacey forced herself onto her elbows to stare in disbelief at what she could now see in the mirror. She could no longer see herself, but a young man. He had thick, dark, unruly hair, and the lower half of his face was covered in stubble. He wore what appeared to be thick, black sunglasses. They looked more like blinders, so even from the sides his eyes were hidden from view. His hands were covered in a fine coating of dark hair, his fingers were long and capped by ivory nails. Despite his eyes being hidden, and the hair that covered his claw-like hands, Lacey could see that the man on the other side of the mirror couldn't be very much older than herself – no more than twenty-two years in age, perhaps.

As Lacey lay in the snow, just inches from the mirror and staring into it, she could see that it wasn't only the young man she found so curious, but the image in the mirror appeared to be see-sawing up and down and side-to-side, as though it were moving at great speed.

"Faster!" the guy shouted, leaning backwards.

Lacey pulled herself up into a kneeling position, ignoring the wet snow that was soaking her jeans. Peering into the mirror, she noticed that the guy on the other side had what appeared to be a set of reins wrapped around his fists.

He pulled on these with all his strength and roared, "Faster! Move faster, can't you! Faster!"

Lacey climbed to her feet, mesmerised by what was unfolding on the other side of the mirror. As if being coaxed forward by an invisible pair of hands, Lacey inched closer to it. Millimetres away now, she saw that the man was sitting atop of what looked like an ancient stagecoach. Lacey blinked, trying to make sense of what she was seeing. The stagecoach was being pulled by a quartet of sleek, black horses.

Lacey watched as he glanced back over

his shoulder, his unkempt hair flicking and blowing all about his face. And with his head turned to the side, Lacey could see that the tips of the young man's ears were pointed. From this angle, the young man looked very wolfish. He faced front again on top of the carriage, and whipped the reins, urging the horses onwards.

"*Faster! Faster!*" he yelled. *"They've nearly caught us!"*

Then, sensing he was being watched, the young man turned to look straight at Lacey. Releasing one of the reins, he thrust a claw-like hand toward her and bellowed, "If you want to save your sister's life, come with me!" He grinned as if he were insane and Lacey could see that his front incisors were pointed, like fangs. "What are you waiting for, Lacey Swift? Are you coming with me or not?"

Lacey considered the question for a moment. The chance to save her twin sister, Thea, was too tempting. But if she took the guy's hand and went through the mirror, what would she be stepping into? She stole a quick look over her shoulder and back in the direction of her uncle's house. Above the treetops and in the distance, Lacey saw what she believed to be torchlight arcing back and forth through the night sky. With her heart turning over in her chest, Lacey feared that it was her uncle, come in search for her. What choice did she have? Stay in the woods and be captured by her uncle and taken back to his house where he would probably kill her, or risk stepping into the mirror and join the young man who sat atop a stagecoach? Neither choice seemed appealing to her.

She faced front. Before she had the chance to decide what she would do, the young man reached out of the mirror with one hand and grabbed her.

With a scream trapped in the back of her throat, Lacey was pulled into the mirror.

Chapter Three

Lacey looked back over her shoulder. The mirror she had been dragged through shattered into a thousand glittering shards or more. Each one disappeared on the wind like glitter, leaving behind the white glare of a sun that now beat down on her in seething hot rays. Just as the icy snow flurries had stung her face, the heat from the sun prickled her flesh like cactus spikes.

Spinning round, Lacey found herself sitting atop the stagecoach, which raced across a hard, flat surface. The ground was bleach-white and arid, cracked and blistered like a corpse left too long in the burning sun. Ahead in the distance, Lacey could see mountains and a forest that stretched across the horizon like a dark smudge. The stagecoach hurtled toward it, pulled by four black horses, spraying up a trail of dust from beneath their hooves. The horses' bodies were muscular and their flesh rippled beneath a coat of sleek and shiny hair. Their manes flowed out behind them in thick waves.

Seated at the front of the carriage, Lacey shot a sideways glance at her new and unfamiliar companion. "How dare you!" she shouted at him over the clatter of the horses' hooves and the roar of the turning wheels of the stagecoach. "You had no right to grab hold of me and pull me..."

"Don't you want to save your sister?" the young man yelled back at her, his wavy hair flowing as they raced across the desert.

"Of course..."

"Then quit complaining!"

"Who are you?" she asked.

"Abraham – or Abe. I don't mind. Whatever you prefer," the guy said, glancing over his shoulder. He looked at Lacey from behind his black glasses. "Do me a favour, don't just sit there looking all shocked and amazed, do something useful."

Starring into Abe's thick, black glasses as if trying to see the eyes hidden behind them, Lacey said, "Do what, exactly?"

Without saying anything, Abe nodded in the direction back over his shoulder.

Spinning round, Lacey was so shocked by what she could now see racing across the desert behind them, she nearly fell from her seat and the stagecoach. "What are they?" she gasped over the thunder of the horses' hooves and their incessant neighing.

Just feet from the rear wheels of the stagecoach were four giant wolves. The wolves were freakishly big. Nearly as big as the horses pulling the stagecoach.

"Don't just sit there with your thumbs up your arse, *shoot them!"* Abe shouted.

"Shoot them?" Lacey gasped. "Shoot them with what?"

"These," Abe said, reaching down and pulling what appeared to be a gun belt from beneath the seat. He thrust it into her hands.

Lacey looked down. There were two holsters made of leather, which housed two weird-looking crossbows. They were no bigger than regular pistols and made from a black metal. "What... how... why have you given me these guns... where did they come from?" Lacey yelled over the sound of the high-pitched neighing coming from the horses up front.

"Does it matter where they came from?" Abe shouted. "Just shoot the Wolf-gatherers or we're going to die!"

She had no real idea what the Wolf-gatherers were, but she suspected Abe was referring to the giant wolves that were leaping and snarling just inches behind the spinning wheels of the stagecoach. Lacey stared at Abe.

"Don't just sit there admiring me, I know you've never seen a guy like me before, but now isn't the time to go all girlie on me. You can check me out later."

"There's nothing girlie about me!" Lacey said, feeling affronted by Abe's remarks. She could take perfectly good care of herself. Her escape from her uncle had been going remarkably well until she had been yanked through that mirror. She slid the crossbows from their holsters and cringed. She didn't know how to shoot. She'd never held a crossbow or gun before. Feeling foolish, she glanced at Abe and said, "I don't know how to shoot."

Abe grinned back at her, his fangs white and gleaming in the sun. And although she couldn't see his eyes, Lacey suspected that they were smiling, too. "What's to know? You just pull the triggers!" He faced front again, and whipped the horses' reins. "Faster! Come on, faster!"

The stagecoach lurched from side to side like a baby taking its first steps. Standing, Lacey fixed the belt about her waist. She drew the crossbows, then took aim. But before firing a shot, she wobbled and almost lost her balance. The stagecoach hit an uneven piece of ground and lurched forward, its back wheels lifting from the earth. Staggering like someone in the dark, Lacey fired one of the crossbows, releasing a shot that went whizzing over Abe's head.

"Don't shoot at me! You're supposed to be shooting at *them!*" Abe shouted, jabbing one claw-like hand back over his shoulder.

Lacey glared at him. "Don't you dare shout at me! I've told you I don't know how to shoot. It's not like I've ever done anything like this before. I don't even know what I'm doing here or where *here* is. You had no right to grab hold of me and pull me..."

"Jeez, don't you talk a lot," Abe cut over her. "How about you save your bitching and whining until later – like much later..."

"I'm not whining," Lacey snapped at him.

"Just shoot!" Abe snarled.

"Dickhead," Lacey mumbled beneath her breath. Standing at the front of the stagecoach, one knee resting on the wooden seat for support, Lacey screwed one eye shut and took aim at the giant wolves. She squeezed down on the triggers. The crossbows thundered in her fists like cannons, this time in the direction of their pursuers.

Small, razor-sharp stakes shot from the end of the crossbows and screamed through the desert sky. One missed, but another sliced into one of the giant wolves. A spray of blood erupted into the air like an exploding water-bomb. The wolf stumbled and rolled forward, crashing into the hard-packed ground. The wolf rolled over and over in the sand, sending up a cloud of dust. Lacey watched as the dust settled, and to her horror, she could see that where the giant wolf had come to rest was now a man. He lay dead on his back, the stake she had fired protruding from his chest. Black blood covered the front of the denim shirt he wore. The man didn't look very much older than herself, but a lot like Abe. He had thick, bushy side whiskers and long, unkempt hair.

"What the fuck!" Lacey cried, glancing at Abe.

"What the what?" Abe said, looking at her from behind the thick, black glasses he wore.

"That wolf... the thing I just shot," Lacey said, struggling to gather her thoughts and form a coherent sentence. "It was a man. I've just killed someone."

"You've killed a monster – not a man," Abe said, facing front again, whipping the reins and urging the horses to run faster and faster.

"But he looked like you – a lot like you!" Lacey yelled over the howls of the wolves that still pursued the stagecoach.

Abe snapped his head around to face her once more. "He was nothing like me," he snarled, top lip curling up so she could see his fangs. "I'm not a Wolf-gatherer."

She stared at him. "So, what are you?"

"Stop looking at me and keep your eyes on *them!*" Abe warned, glancing back at the massive wolves. But his warning came too late.

One of the wolves had drawn level with the stagecoach. The wolf began to ram its huge head into the side of the carriage. The back of the vehicle spun to one side, sending Lacey flying over the edge of the coach.

Corkscrewing through the air, Lacey squeezed her eyes shut and waited for the explosion of pain to tear through her body as she hit the ground that raced below. But the pain never came. Opening her eyes, Lacey blinked as the cracked earth whizzed past just inches from her face. Glancing upwards, she saw that one of her boots had been caught in the frame of the stagecoach.

"Abe, help me!" Lacey cried, hanging upside down on the outside of the carriage. Looking to her right, the gigantic paws of one wolf slammed into the ground next to her like a hammer. It jerked its giant head forward, opening its jaws and lunging at her face. Hot drool sprayed from its snout and spattered against her. The wolf was so close that she could feel its breath warm on her face. Gritting her teeth, Lacey twisted her body as she tried to lean away from the creature. Dust blew up into her eyes like gunpowder. She didn't want to kill the wolf if it meant killing another man, but she didn't want to die either. The wolf snarled and barked as it snapped its mighty jaws open and closed just inches from her face. Within another bound the wolf would be closing its ferocious jaws about her throat. Squinting, Lacey raised her left arm and took aim at it with one of the crossbows.

Almost blind through the swirling grit and dust spraying up from beneath the stagecoach wheels, she squeezed on the trigger. Her arm recoiled like a rattlesnake as the stake exploded from the barrel of the crossbow. An ear-splitting screech cut through the air as the sharp wooden stake whizzed toward the wolf.

Opening her eyes, Lacey watched the wolf tumbling across the desert, its long tail flipping back and forth. But as the creature came to settle in the sand, she could see that it no longer looked like a wolf, but a man. The stake she had fired jutted from his eye socket. Blood streamed down the young man's face.

"I'm sorry," Lacey whispered.

Looking up at her entangled boot, Lacey could see her foot was coming loose. Realising she was in danger of falling to her certain death beneath the wheels of the carriage, Lacey began to scream. There was no sign of Abe responding to her cries. Sensing that she was going to have to save herself, she looked around in desperation, searching for something, anything to grab that would help her lever herself back on top of the carriage. Seeing the handle of the stagecoach door, she grabbed for it like a drowning woman. Knowing that if she could reach it and get the door open, she could climb inside to safety.

Holstering her crossbows and using what little strength she had left, Lacey arched her back and tried to pull herself forward. Clenching her teeth and eyes watering, she managed to heave herself up, fingers clawing for the coach door handle inches from her grasp.

"I can do it!" she yelled aloud, willing herself on.

Screwing her eyes shut, she made one last grab for the handle, and to her utter delight and relief, she felt her fingers curl around its metal surface. Then someone gripped her wrist, yanking her hand free.

Snapping open her eyes, Lacey looked up into Abe's face.

"Have you lost your freaking mind?" Lacey yelled. "Do you want me to die?"

Staring at Lacey from behind his thick, black lensed glasses, Abe flashed his fangs. "Here you go again, moan, moan, moan. Don't you ever stop to take a breath?" He yanked on Lacey's wrist, pulling her back to safety.

"I wasn't moaning," Lacey snapped, pulling her wrist free of his grip. The scar was aching again. She rubbed it. "I just didn't want you to drop me... and..."

"And what?" Abe cut over her.

"And that was another man I just killed back there," she shouted at him.

"He wasn't a man," Abe said. "Not like the kind of man you're thinking of."

"Like what then?" she demanded to know.

"I don't have time to drill down into the finer points right now," Abe said, turning away. "We'll discuss it later..."

Lacey grabbed his arm. "You'll tell me now!"

"I don't have time," he said, brushing Lacey's hand from his arm. "We need to get him to safety. That's why I didn't want you to open the carriage door because he might die," Abe said, scampering over the carriage roof and dropping back down on the seat.

"Who will die? Who's *he*?" Lacey asked, sitting beside him again.

"You'll see," Abe replied. Then, whipping the horses' reins again, he shouted, "Faster!"

Looking back over her shoulder, and fearing that Abe might expect her to take aim at the two remaining wolves that chased them, Lacey was surprised and somewhat relieved to see they had begun to slow. They were no longer bounding after them, but had slowed their pace to a saunter.

"Why are they slowing down?" Lacey asked.

"Because we're heading into the forest," Abe said.

Lacey shot Abe a sideways glance. "Why won't they enter the forest?"

"Because of the dead people," Abe answered, whipping the reins again and heading into the forest.

Chapter Four

As her twin sister had stepped through the mirror in the woods, Thea Swift peered over the top of the blanket and watched her bedroom door swing open. She knew at once who was about to enter the room by the tall shadow that spilt across the wall like a splash of black ink. Creeping from behind the door, her uncle, Victor Swift, crept into the room. Balanced on one of his bony hands was a silver tray. From her position on the bed, Thea couldn't see what was on the tray. She didn't need to – she knew that her uncle was bringing her afternoon dose of medicine.

Placing the tray on the dressing table, Victor surveyed Thea with his beady-black eyes. Without taking his stare from her, he opened a small wooden box. From it, he removed a black object. It was about the size of a dice. Taking a glass from the tray, Victor offered Thea the black-coloured pill and water.

"I don't want it," Thea croaked, her throat still feeling blistered and sore from the dose of medicine she had been forced to swallow that morning.

"Take it," her uncle coaxed, thrusting the

pill toward her lips. "It will make you feel better."

"They make me feel worse!" Thea protested, pulling the blanket up over her mouth.

Seeing this, Victor's thin, bloodless lips twisted into a grimace then contorted into a smile, as he tried to mask his displeasure. Gripping the pill between thumb and forefinger, he placed the glass back onto the tray and eased himself down onto the bed next to his niece.

"You must take your medicine, Thea, or you may well die," he said in a soothing voice, which caused gooseflesh to break out over Thea's flesh.

Eyeing him with suspicion, Thea looked into his dark eyes that sat in nets of deep wrinkles. "What's wrong with me?" she asked him.

"I'm not sure," he said. "I've consulted all of my medical books and I've never seen anything quite like it. Strange. Very *strange*," he added, his tongue darting from between his lips.

Thea thought back to the day she had first become ill. Thea remembered it well. She and her twin sister had been living with their uncle at his isolated cottage in the southwest of England since their early teens – since they had buried their parents. Thea and Lacey had always though their uncle to be somewhat weird – creepy – but they had no other family to raise them. So they got on with their lives as best they could. Her strange and sudden illness had started with stomach cramps, just a few days after joining the local college. The pains had felt as if some creature had been let loose inside her and was tearing away at her innards with razor-sharp claws. Then the headaches came and they were so severe, she wondered if her head wasn't going to explode. Lacey had fallen ill a year later and they both had to leave college so that their uncle could nurse them. He had suggested that they be moved to separate bedrooms, so as not to spread the infection, if that was what it was.

But their uncle had come to the rescue. He was a doctor, after all, well not so much a doctor but a *medicine man* – as he would so often refer to himself. Her uncle hadn't been around much when she and her sister had been small children, spending most of his time travelling to weird and wonderful countries. On his return, he would visit her father claiming to have found a cure for this and a remedy for that.

"This will make me rich beyond my wildest dreams," he had once boasted to her father, holding aloft a bottle, which looked as if it were filled with nothing more than dirty bathwater.

"What does it do?" Thea and Lacey's father had asked from behind his newspaper.

"What does it do?!" Victor had groaned in despair at his brother, Edward. "It's a cure!"

"For what?" Edward had asked. Again, he didn't look up from his newspaper. Edward found his older brother an irritation and pretentious. Why couldn't Victor have become a proper doctor – a doctor who actually cured people and made them feel better?

Standing before Edward, Victor glared at him with his piercing stare. Seeing that his younger brother wasn't the slightest bit interested – as he had heard similar stories many times before – Victor said, "Oh what's the point!" He then skulked from the house and back to his bleak-looking cottage hidden away amongst the cliffs in Cornwall.

And it was that cottage where Thea now lay, feverish and in pain as her uncle tried to convince her to take more of his revolting medicine.

Pulling the lip of the blanket away from Thea's face, Victor placed the black gleaming pill against her dry and flaky lips.

"Go on, take your medicine," he whispered.

Puckering up her lips, Thea shook her head from side to side. If she'd had the strength to do so, Thea would have thrown back the blankets, and run.

"Don't you want to get better?" he asked her, a twinge of irritation evident in his voice.

Thea wearily shook her head in reluctance and wheezed. "I'm nineteen now and you can't make me do anything that I don't want to do."

"And I'm your uncle and you have been left in my charge, so you will do as I tell you," Victor said. The irritation he had earlier tried to mask now making his voice sound hostile. "Your mother and father saw fit to let me raise you since you and your sister were both thirteen."

"Only because they died – and besides, we're no longer children," Thea said, looking into his eyes. She could see they were black and cold – lifeless. She couldn't bear to look at him and wished that her father was still alive. He had been a gentle man with kind eyes and a lopsided grin, which lit up his face like candlelight. Turning her head away, she buried her cheek into the pillow. She did this not to break her uncle's heartless stare, but to hide the hot, sticky tears that now ran the length of her ashen face.

Before the pillowcase had soaked up even one of her tears, Victor curled his long, gnarled fingers around her face, forcing Thea to look at him. Tightening his grip, he stretched her mouth open. Being too weak to resist him, Victor was able to easily drop the pill into her mouth and force it shut.

Desperate not to swallow the pill, Thea's eyes began to bulge in their sockets. The pill began to melt in her mouth, filling it with an acid-like substance that scorched the inside of her cheeks and tongue.

"Don't fight it," Victor soothed, but however hard he tried to make his voice comforting, his eyes betrayed his true feelings as they danced in their wet-looking sockets.

Thea fought to push the pill back toward her lips with her tongue. But it had almost dissolved. To do so hurt too much, and her mouth began to taste of rusty copper as it started to fill with blood. Realising she would have to swallow the pill, Thea closed her eyes and gulped.

Seeping to the back of her mouth, the dissolving pill scorched her tonsils and then disappeared down her throat. Shaking her uncle's hand free, Thea buried her chin into her chest, leant forward, and swallowed hard. As the thick liquid made its way down her throat Thea wondered if it was a similar feeling to swallowing broken glass.

It made its way through her body, her chest growing warm then hot. Thea's lungs felt as if they were on fire. When the rancid liquid reached her stomach, she felt a rush of hot bile in her throat, and then the pain began to subside. A wave of tiredness swept over her as it always did after taking one of Victor's pills. She lowered her head onto the pillow and fought the urge to close her eyes.

Scooping up the tray, Victor headed back across the room. As he reached the door, he heard Thea whisper.

"Where's Lacey? I want to see my sister."

"Lacey is too unwell to pay you a visit. Perhaps when she is feeling better," her uncle grinned back before sneaking beyond the door and closing it behind him.

Turning to look through the lattice window across from her bed, Thea doubted if she would ever see her identical twin sister again. They had always been close – had a strong connection between them. Thea had always known when Lacey was happy or sad, what she was thinking, and what she was going to say next. And as Thea struggled to keep her eyes open and stay strong, she sensed that Lacey was no longer close by – that she had escaped their uncle and was now very far away. Such a thought should have pleased Thea, knowing that her sister had managed to get away from the danger Victor posed. But as Thea's eyes closed and she fell into a deep sleep, she sensed that her sister – wherever she might be – faced an even greater danger.

Chapter Five

Yanking on the reins, Abe brought the horses to a halt amongst the trees. Lacey glanced over her shoulder and saw the two remaining giant wolves roaming back and forth just beyond the treeline. The wolves threw back their colossal heads and howled. The sight and sound of them made Lacey feel anxious. Not only because they were abnormally big wolves, but because in some way, and somehow, they appeared to be men too. She feared that if they followed her and Abe into the forest she would be expected to kill them and she wasn't sure that she could, now that she knew that they were half man, half creature. But if they were going to kill her, then she would have to find the nerve to shoot, whether she was expected to or not.

"Are you sure they won't follow us into the forest?" Lacey asked Abe.

Abe placed one finger to his mouth. "Shhh," he said, glancing up into the treetops as if waiting for something.

Unlike the desert they had just raced across, the forest was dark and just the smallest chinks of light cut through the rich canopy above them. Being amongst the shadows of the trees had an eerie feel to it, and Lacey could hear her own heart thumping in her ears.

"Here they come!" Abe suddenly said, clambering from the roof of the stagecoach.

"Who's coming?" Lacey asked, jumping to the ground. She followed Abe around the side of the coach.

Before Abe could say anything else, the forest began to wail with deep groaning sounds that vibrated off the trees and the earth beneath their feet. Looking round, Lacey shivered as the sounds grew louder. Branches began to rustle and snap, like breaking bones.

Lacey's eyes grew wide. "What's happening?" she asked above the deafening sounds.

Pulling open the carriage door, Abe turned to look at Lacey from behind his dark glasses. "Don't just stand there, help me get him out." He then climbed into the stagecoach, disappearing from view.

Leaves and pine needles showered her from above like green raindrops. Looking at the trees, Lacey wondered if she wouldn't, in fact, be safer in the company of her uncle than inside the forest with Abe. It seemed that she had escaped one nightmare only to find herself in another. Lacey had no idea who *he* was or even *where* she was. So much had happened since stepping through the mirror in the woods, that she'd had barely a chance to make much sense of anything. There was still a part of her that believed she was dreaming – that she hadn't, in fact, escaped from her uncle's house and was still under his influence, suffering the weirdest kinds of hallucinations due to the strange and poisonous medicine he had been giving to her.

Through the trees, Lacey could see the freakish wolves prowling back and forth along the edge of the treeline. One of them suddenly reared onto its back legs as if it had been scared somehow. But what could have frightened such a wolf? She had no idea.

Lacey saw what at first appeared to look like mist and smoke. It seeped down from the branches overhead in wispy tendrils. As it touched the forest floor, the smoke, if that's what it was, began to take a human-like form. The ghostly figures were naked and painfully thin. Although they were transparent, Lacey could see that some were men, others women. Male or female, their hair was matted in rough clumps, and their faces were screwed up – tortured-looking – as if they were in agonizing pain. These humanlike apparitions floated between the trees at speed toward the treeline. But there they stopped, as if mindful not to venture out into the hot glare of the desert. They swooped back and forth, each of them releasing a heart-wrenching and agonizing sob. It sounded as if these lost souls were in perpetual pain and misery.

The whole forest now seemed to be alive with these ghostly figures. They dripped from the trees and some seeped up like fog from beneath the ground. It was like the dead were rising from their graves. Their groans and moans filled the air like the solemn beat of a drum. Without thinking, Lacey placed a hand on the hilt of one of her crossbows, preparing to defend herself should one of the spirit-like people come for her.

"You're wasting your time. You're not going to kill them," Abe said from inside the stagecoach. "Didn't I tell you that they are already dead?"

Lacey wheeled round. She peered into the dark confines of the carriage. "What are they, ghosts?"

"Not exactly, but similar," Abe said, his voice gruff as it floated out of the darkness at her.

The earth beneath Lacey's trainers began to tremor and the horses began to whinny with fright. They started to edge forward, pulling the stagecoach deeper into the forest. Failing to notice the stagecoach moving away, Lacey looked in horror as a set of grey and smoky fingers slithered from beneath the earth inches from her feet. She staggered backwards as the fingers were followed by an arm, a pair of shoulders, and then a head. The ghostly creature twisted and turned before looking up at Lacey.

The scream locked in the back of her throat threatened to suffocate her. Up close, she could see the face of the phantom was grotesque. The opaque flesh covering its face looked scorched and blistered. The ghost released an agonising groan from the back of its throat as it reached out at Lacey with a pair of fleshless hands. The fingers were knotted like twisted tree roots.

Abe appeared in the carriage doorway in search of Lacey. He looked down at the creature crawling over the earth toward Lacey, then back at her. "Will you stop messing around and come give me a hand."

Hearing his voice, Lacey shot a look over her shoulder and toward the carriage. "I'm not messing about! This is serious!"

"Yeah, and so is this, now take his legs," Abe said, diving back into the stagecoach.

"You've done nothing but criticise me. I admit, you're not like any guy I've ever met before, but your attitude is beginning to get on my bloody nerves," she fumed, stepping around the creature crawling through the earth toward her. Without warning, a pair of booted feet were thrust into the open doorway at her.

"Take hold and pull," Abe said from somewhere in the darkness of the carriage.

Sensing that any objection would be pointless, Lacey took hold of the legs dangling out of the carriage and pulled. As she did, a semi-conscious man appeared in the carriage doorway. Abe was cradling him in his arms. The groaning was closer now, and looking over her shoulder, Lacey could see a ghostly form floating toward them. Its arms were outstretched and its hands were clawing at the air.

"Don't just stand there gawping, Lacey, give me some help here," Abe grumbled.

Doubling her efforts, Lacey helped Abe heave the unconscious man from the carriage. "I think we should get out of here – and quick," Lacey said, glancing once more in the direction of the ghost.

"It won't hurt us," Abe assured her, pulling the unconscious man's legs free from her grasp. He swooped the man up into his arms, then onto his shoulders.

"How can you be so sure it won't hurt us?" Lacey said, the phantom inches from them.

"Because *he's* with us," Abe said, gesturing to the man he had draped over his shoulder.

Then looking at Lacey, he added, "There's a bag in the carriage – it belongs to you."

Lacey frowned. "A bag? What's in it?" She poked her head into the carriage.

"Your clothes," Abe said.

She glanced over her shoulder at him. "My clothes? But I'm wearing my clothes."

"These are new ones – boots and stuff," Abe said.

"But I don't want new clothes," Lacey said, picking up the cloth sack she had found in the carriage. "I like the clothes I'm wearing."

Abe grinned. "All girls like to get new clothes, don't they?"

"I'm not a girl," Lacey shot back. "I'm a woman."

Abe cocked one bushy eyebrow at her. "And *women* don't like new clothes?"

"Well, yes… but my point is that…"

"Moan, moan, moan," Abe sighed, turning his back on Lacey and setting off into the woods, carrying the young man over his shoulders.

Realising that it was pointless to argue with Abe, she hoisted the sack into her arms and set off after him. Now that the man was free of the carriage, Lacey looked at him. Like herself and Abe, this man was young, no older than twenty. He looked very undernourished. His skin looked burnt and blistered, and a fine sheen of perspiration covered his brow and cheeks. He looked like a waxwork that had started to melt. The young man's eyes rolled in their sockets and he murmured as if talking in his sleep. Thanks to her uncle's medicine, Lacey had spent much of her time in a catatonic state, suffering hallucinations, and she had no doubt that the young man was delirious. His hair was thick and black. He was dressed in a long, dark leather coat that had a hood, dark trousers, black boots, and leather fingerless gloves.

"Who is he?" Lacey whispered.

Abe pulled the hood down over the young man's head. "He's one of *them*," Abe said, nodding in the direction of the ghost-like man they had left swooping about in the air behind them.

Chapter Six

"What do you mean he's one of *them*?" Lacey asked, following Abe deeper into the forest, where the trees grew close and even less light shone down through the canopy of leaves overhead.

"He's a Blood Runner," Abe said, carrying the young man draped over his shoulder.

Lacey jogged to keep up, crossbows bouncing against her thighs. Even though the wolfish young man was carrying the other, he moved with such speed and agility that she had trouble keeping up with him. Lacey was now grateful that she had managed to regain much of her strength before escaping from her uncle's home. Since stepping through the mirror, she had felt stronger and more vibrant than she could ever remember feeling before.

'What's a *Blood Runner*?' Lacey asked, quickening her stride to keep up with Abe.

"They're the night-folk. They live by night, hiding away from the sun by day – it can kill them," Abe explained.

Lacey thought for a moment about what she had heard. "We have creatures like that back home... in my world," Lacey said, ducking to avoid a low-hanging branch. "But they're just in stories... horror movies. We call them vampires."

"Are you so sure they're just stories?" Abe asked, glancing at Lacey through the dark lenses he wore. She wished she could see his eyes, so she could get a better sense of the young man behind them.

"Of course they're just stories," Lacey now puffed, fighting to stay level with Abe.

"I hate to be the one who tells you this," Abe grinned, "but vampires are real. They are the *Blood Runners* who have passed through the mirrors from our world and into yours. In our world, they are just Blood Runners, but in your world they become *vampires.*"

They reached a small clearing and Abe came to a sudden stop. He sniffed the air before setting off again, shouting over his shoulder, "Follow me."

Lacey watched as her strange companion set off at speed. "So what does that make you? A werewolf?" she called after him, half-joking but fearing his answer. She ran to keep up with him.

"Only in your world," Abe said. "Here, I'm a Moon Howler. My surname is Sandulf, which means true wolf."

"And those others?" Lacey asked.

"What others?"

"The giant wolves – the Wolf-gatherers – the wolves that turned into men, are they like you? Are they Moon Howlers?"

"No," Abe said. "We are part of the same species – werewolves, as you like to call us – but the Moon Howlers are different from the Wolf-gatherers."

"How so?"

"We don't eat humans you'll be glad to know," Abe said, shifting the young man onto his other shoulder.

"How do I know you don't eat humans?" Lacey said.

"You're still alive, aren't you?"

"But you might eat me later," she said.

He shot her a mischievous grin. "Don't get ahead of yourself, Lacey Swift, we've only just met – don't you think we should get to know each other first, before we get intimate?"

"In your dreams," she shot back, annoyed that her cheeks had flushed red at his comment. "You know perfectly well what I meant."

"And you should know you're perfectly safe with me," Abe said.

"But that's the whole point," Lacey said. "I don't know you. I don't know where I am, or what I'm doing here."

Without saying another word, Abe was racing ahead, leading Lacey deep into the forest.

This has got to be a dream – the result of some brain fever brought on by those disgusting pills Victor force-fed me, Lacey thought. But whether a dream or not – she didn't want to leave it or this world just yet. Despite Abe being somewhat cocky and looking like some kind of wolf-man, she quite liked him – was fascinated by him and the stories he had to tell. And although she had found herself in several life-threatening situations since stepping through the mirror, she was still alive. She hadn't been eaten by Abe or anyone or anything, yet. In the back of her mind, she reminded herself that however terrifying some nightmares became, they were nothing more than dreams, and she would wake up before she died – that's what happened in dreams. She always woke up before she hit the ground. And if waking up meant finding herself once more lying weak and ill in her bed – imprisoned by her uncle – then she would rather stay asleep for a little while longer, dreaming that she was racing through a forest with the strangest young man she had ever met.

They ran in silence, Lacey trying to make sense of this new world and what Abe had told her. But if this wasn't a dream and was very real, why was she here? But more importantly, where was *here*?

Abe reached another small clearing and

stopped. The area was circular in shape, and at its centre there was a small, burnt-out fire. Surrounding this were several large rocks that looked as big as chairs. Abe carried the young man over to one of these large stones and settled him against it. Abe then disappeared into the nearby undergrowth and reappeared carrying an armful of branches and twigs. He began to pile these on top of the burnt-out campfire. Lacey cradled the sack of new clothes to her chest.

Abe glanced up at her. "Put the clothes on."

"No," she said.

"Why not?"

"I'm not getting undressed here – in front of you."

"Scared I might be tempted to eat you?" he grinned, before turning his attention back to the fire he was building. "Besides, I can't see you –not really. I'm almost blind, that's why I wear the dark glasses."

Reaching down, Lacey snatched up a nearby stone and tossed it at Abe. Without a moment's hesitation, he shot out one hand and caught the stone.

"Liar!" Lacey scowled.

Abe began to chuckle to himself as she turned her back on him and headed out of the clearing and back into the forest. When she was far enough away from Abe so as not to be seen by him, Lacey set the sack down at the foot of a nearby tree. She opened up the neck of the sack and reached inside. She pulled out a pair of knee-high black leather boots, a long, black coat with hood, and a pair of trousers. Both items of clothing were also cut from leather. There was a white shirt with lace at the collar and cuffs. Glancing back over her shoulder, she spied through the trees and could see that Abe was still sitting before the fire he was building in the centre of the clearing. Confident that she was quite alone, Lacey undressed and put on the new clothes. They fit perfectly, as if they had indeed been intended for her all along. She fixed the gun belt about her waist and tied the holsters about each thigh with their leather straps and silver buckles. A series of silver clasps like fishhooks lined the front of her long, flowing coat, and she secured them together.

She reached again into the sack and retrieved a pair of black gloves and what looked like some kind of leather sheath. She put the gloves on, but wasn't sure what to do with the last remaining item. Down one side of it was a series of strings, like shoelaces. Along the other side there was what looked like a series of knives and blades. As she held it up for a closer inspection, she realised that it was a leather gauntlet that fitted about her wrist and forearm. Lacey strapped it about her left arm, and just like the clothing, it was a perfect fit. She raised her arm and took a closer look at the knives and what appeared to be small daggers. Just above her wrist, there was a copper circular housing. In the centre, there was a hole where something could be attached. But what, Lacey had no idea. With her other hand, she slowly turned the copper dial. To her surprise it made a humming noise. This was followed by a series of clicking sounds as the blades, knives, and daggers that covered the gauntlet flicked open and up. They jutted from the gauntlet, fierce and sharp. Lacey thought that her arm now looked like the most dangerous and menacing Swiss Army Knife she had ever seen. She turned the dial again, and the knives and blades began to spin around, open and close, thrust in and out. What kind of weapon was it, and why did she need it? She wondered. She turned the copper dial once more and the razor-sharp instruments folded away, lying flat against the gauntlet once more.

Dressed in her new attire, Lacey headed out of the forest and back into the clearing. Abe heard her coming and looked back over his shoulder.

"Wow," he said, mouth falling open. "You really do look good enough to eat... and believe me, I'm a slow eater…"

"Enough already!" Lacey said, pointing one finger at him, although it was nice to be complimented, but perhaps not in such a salacious way. It hadn't happened often – if ever. Where had she ever gone to meet anyone who might admire her? She had spent much of the last few years of her life drugged and dazed in her bedroom. Not wanting to give Abe the opportunity to make another lewd comment, she looked across the clearing at the young man who had curled himself into a ball next to the large plinth of stone. He shook as if he was freezing cold. From where Lacey stood, the young man looked sick and feverish.

"What's his name?" Lacey asked Abe.

"Marco Lamia," he replied, turning his attention back to the fire that he hadn't yet lit.

"Is he ill?"

"Kind of."

"What happened to him?"

Abe patted the pockets of his blue denim shirt and then rummaged through those that covered his worn-looking jeans. As Lacey stood on the opposite side of the clearing and watched him, she realised, for the first time, that Abe's feet were shoeless. Just like his fingers, his toes were long and covered in thick, brown hair.

"Marco was out in the sun for too long,"

Abe replied, after finding what it was he had been searching his pockets for. He pulled out a small wooden box from his trouser pocket. Flipping it open, Abe took out a match, struck it alight, and then held the flame to the branches and sticks placed on the campfire.

"If the sun can kill him, what was he doing out in the desert?" Lacey asked, moving to the centre of the clearing and sitting on the ground near the fire Abe had set.

"We were looking for you," Abe said, stoking the fire with a long, twisted stick until it was fully ablaze. He then glanced at Lacey, the flames reflecting off the lenses of the dark glasses he wore.

Lacey frowned at him. "You were looking for me?"

"Well, not exactly. We were looking for the mirror that you would come through."

"But how did you know I would come?"

"That was the problem, you see. We knew you would eventually come across a mirror, but we couldn't be sure *when* and exactly *where*. So, every night for the last month, Marco and I have travelled across the desert looking for your mirror to appear. And last night we saw it, shining like a star just above the desert floor. But before we could reach it, the sun had crept up on us, and then those Wolf-gatherers spotted us and made chase." Reaching into his jeans pocket again, Abe pulled out a piece of twine. He used this to pull his wild-looking hair into a ponytail at the base of his neck. Now that his hair was pulled away from the sides of his face, Lacey could see it more clearly. She thought that, apart from his pointed ears, he didn't look so wolfish and just like any other guy. Although his eyes were still hidden from her behind the thick, black glasses, she thought that he was good-looking – in an offbeat kind of way.

"What happened when those Wolf-gatherers started to chase you?" Lacey asked, keen to know more about him and his friend Marco and why they had been searching for her – for her mirror.

"I needed Marco to fight those Wolf-gatherers off as I raced toward you," Abe started to explain. "I had to keep the stagecoach on a fine line because if I'd over-steered by just a fraction, I wouldn't have been able to pull you through. Anyway, Marco tried to fight off those Wolf-gatherers for far too long." He glanced over at his friend, who was completely hidden beneath the long coat he wore, and added, "Marco fought bravely, though, and even when the sun became unbearable, he stood his ground so we could reach you."

Feeling somewhat guilty that these

strangers had seemingly risked so much for her, even though she did not know them, Lacey glanced over at the young man, who continued to shiver against the large piece of stone.

"Eventually, though," Abe continued, "Marco had to escape into the coach or... he would have..."

As if almost too painful to complete his sentence, Abe stopped talking and continued to prod at the fire that snapped and hissed in front of them.

"But that really doesn't answer my question," Lacey said after a few quiet moments of contemplation. "How did you know I was going to come in the first place?"

"It was only a matter of time," a voice said from behind her.

Turning, Lacey could see a figure standing amongst the trees on the other side of the clearing. Peering into the darkness, Lacey shielded her eyes against the glare of the fire with her hands.

"Who's there?" Lacey called out, a sense of unease creeping over her again.

"It's okay," Abe assured her. "It's just my father come to join us."

Recognising his son's voice, the figure that stood hidden amongst the shadows spoke. "Have the Wolf-gatherers gone?"

"Yes," Abe said, standing to greet his father.

Lacey watched as the man stepped into the clearing. Abe's father was huge; a mountain of a man. He was tall and stocky with shoulders so round and muscular they resembled cannonballs. Just like his son, he had a dark mop of unruly hair, but had bushy side whiskers. He wore blue jeans and a red checked shirt with the sleeves rolled to his elbows. At his side stood a wolf with fur as white as snow. This wolf wasn't abnormal in size like the others Lacey had seen, but it was still an impressive-looking creature, with its long, bushy tail, thick shiny coat of fur, and piercing blue eyes.

As Abe's father stepped into the firelight, the wolf at his side, Lacey noticed the man's eyes. At first glance they looked as if they were jet-black and set in deep, dark sockets which screwed right back into his skull. But on further inspection, Lacey could see that Abe's father didn't have eyes. The darkness surrounding the empty sockets were, in fact, scorch marks. She glanced across the clearing at Abe. She wondered whether his eyes were the same as his father's and the reason why he wore the shades.

In spite of having no eyes, the man stepped into the clearing and strode toward Lacey and Abe. He navigated his way around the large rocks where Marco rested, and stopped just before walking into the fire. At first, Lacey wondered if he had managed to do this by an acute sense of hearing and smell, but then realised that it was the wolf that was leading and guiding the man. Although the creature wasn't on a leash, Lacey could see that it walked so close to Abe's father that his hand continuously brushed against the wolf's fur.

"Good girl, Una," Abe's father said, stooping to pat his guide with one of his giant hands.

A thick, pink tongue slipped from between the wolf's jaws and licked its master's fingers. The wolf sat and Abe's father settled on the ground. Once they were both comfortable, the wolf rested its whiskered snout on its front paws, and Abe's father turned his dead-eyes on Lacey.

"So, Lacey – where shall we start?" he said, his voice deep and grave. "I know, let's talk about your uncle, Victor Swift."

Chapter Seven

Victor Swift stood in the open doorway of his cottage and looked out toward the woods. He swung his torch from side to side and the beam of light arced into the night.

"Lacey!" he hissed into the darkness.

Victor glanced at his wristwatch. It was just before midnight and he hadn't seen his niece, Lacey, since earlier that morning, when he'd gone to her room to give her the medicine. But when he had gone back to administer the evening dose, she was gone.

"Lacey," he called again into the night. "Where are you, you stupid bitch?"

He was annoyed with himself because he should have known that something was up and everything hadn't been quite right when he'd gone to Lacey's room that morning. She had peered over the blankets at him like she always did. Lacey had appeared as pale as ever, but there had been a tone to her voice, that he now knew with hindsight, suggested that she wasn't as drowsy and feeble as she perhaps appeared to have been.

Stopping halfway across the room, Victor

had looked at Lacey with disdain. She had always been more belligerent than her twin sister. Lacey had always had far too much to say for herself. Maybe that's why he had read the situation wrong. Missed the signs. He had grown accustomed to her cockiness. It was the reason that when she had gone down with that cold just after finishing her first year at college and taken to her bed, he had seized on the opportunity to start giving her the pills. He couldn't risk Lacey nor Thea growing independent – making lives for themselves. He had to keep her close – both of them. Thea he had started to poison just after she had joined college. He'd had to be careful. He couldn't risk both sisters falling ill at the same time – the college and the authorities might have grown suspicious.

"Why do you keep giving me and Thea that stuff?" she had asked, as Victor crept across the bedroom toward her.

"What do you know about *anything*?" Victor said, as if he were spitting a vile taste from his mouth.

"I know that those pills aren't making me nor Thea better. They're making us worse," Lacey protested.

On hearing this, Victor placed the tray with the pill and glass of water down on the bedside cabinet. He loomed over Lacey as she lay on her bed. He grimaced. "Listen to me, you piece of shit, who's the doctor around here? Me or you?"

"You're not a doctor," Lacey snapped in defiance, her light blue eyes peering out from over the top of the blanket at him.

"I think you'll find that I'm more than *just* a doctor. I'm a healer!"

"You couldn't heal a cold," Lacey said, knowing that perhaps she was now pushing her luck with Victor – with her captor.

"What did you say?" he spat, his face screwing up into a hideous mask of anger. *"What did you say to me, you ungrateful bitch?"*

Lacey pulled the blanket tighter about her as if it would offer her some form of protection from her uncle. "Why can't you just leave me and my sister alone and get a proper doctor to come and treat us?"

"A proper doctor?" Victor scoffed. "And what would a proper doctor know about real medicine?"

"More than you," Lacey said under her breath.

"Does a so-called *proper* doctor know what I know? Have they seen what I have seen?" he said, his piercing black eyes boring into Lacey. "Have they been trained by the best like I have? Do they know the true power of...?" he stopped mid-outburst as if realising he had perhaps said too much. Victor straightened himself and unscrewed his face. Mustering a twisted smile, he said, "I can assure you that you and your sister are getting the best treatment available. Now why don't you shut the fuck up and take your medicine and be a good girl like your sister, Thea."

Lacey watched Victor take the poisonous black pill and glass of water from the tray. Placing one knee onto the bed, he leant over her, his face so close to hers that she could smell his stale breath.

"I wish my mother and father were still alive. They would have stopped you," Lacey said, turning her face away.

Closing his free hand around her face, he buried his fingers deep into her flesh. He turned her head, forcing her to look at him. With a cruel smile that looked as if his face had been cut from ear to ear, he whispered, "But your parents aren't *here,* are they? They're dead, dead, *dead!*"

Chuckling, he forced Lacey's mouth open with his fingers. She made a gagging noise in the back of her throat as he dropped the pill into her mouth. He then snapped her mouth shut with such force her teeth rattled in their gums. With one of his bony hands clamped over her mouth, he waited long enough for her to have swallowed the pill. Only when Lacey's eyes had started to bulge in their sockets, and her face had begun to turn grey-blue, did Victor release his hand. He climbed from the bed and made his way toward the bedroom door.

"I hate you – you fucking *freak!*" Lacey shouted. "Why couldn't it have been you who had died in that accident?"

"Because I never walk too close to a cliff's edge," he said, stopping in the open doorway and glancing back at her with a smile. "How unfortunate that both your parents slipped and fell to their deaths. I'm just glad that I survived so you and your sister weren't totally alone in this world." Without another word, Victor left the room, laughing so hard he had tears spilling down his cheeks.

That was the last time Victor had seen his niece. When he had returned to her room later that evening, her blankets had been thrown back and she was no longer cowering beneath them. He had searched the house, but she was nowhere to be seen. It was only when he had discovered footprints in the snow heading away from the back of the house and toward the woods that he knew for sure she had escaped him. But it was too dark, the snowfall too heavy to go in search for her. It would have to wait until first light. But he knew that the woods stretched for miles. And in the direction she had set off in, there wasn't a road or town. And what, with the blizzard and the freezing temperature, he knew Lacey wouldn't get far. Come first light, she would have either returned to the house cold and hungry, knowing that her escape was fruitless, or he would find her frozen to death in the woods.

Victor switched off his torch, stepped back into the warmth of the cottage, and closed the door. He went to the living room, where he sat in his favourite chair before the fireplace.

Lacing his long and bony fingers under his chin like a steeple, he closed his eyes and thought about the mirror. He pictured it in his mind until he could see it, tall, gleaming and set in a frame of twisted black iron. Opening his eyes, Victor was pleased to see it there, standing amongst the roaring flames in the fireplace. He could see himself reflected in it as he sat, hands now stretched before the flames, to warm them. Gradually, his reflection began to waver and ripple like water. As the ripples began to dissipate out from the centre of the mirror and toward the frame, another image revealed itself in the glass. On the other side of the mirror there was a stone-clad corridor. Just like the fireplace, orange flames licked from torches that lined the walls of the corridor for as far as the eye could see.

Easing himself out of his favourite chair, Victor stood and crept into the mirror.

Chapter Eight

Abe's father, Fletcher Sandulf, sat by the fire and stroked the wolf, which lay peacefully at his side. The last chinks of daylight had long since faded, and the forest was now in total darkness. If it hadn't been for the flames dancing in front of them, Lacey doubted she would have been able to see anything at all.

Abe sat beside Lacey, and Marco lay bundled beneath his coat against the stones on the opposite side of the clearing. Marco's hood had ridden back to reveal some of his face that wasn't masked by shadow. His eyes were closed and he rested his head on his gloved hands as if they were pillows. Lacey noticed that Marco had stopped shivering and the only movement he now made was the rhythmic rise and fall of his chest as he breathed deeply in and out.

Looking away from Marco, Lacey turned to face Abe's father and said, "Where am I?" Although she was desperate to know how he knew her uncle, *where am I?* was the question she wanted answered the most.

Turning his empty eye sockets on Lacey, Fletcher said, "You're in the Mirror Realm."

"What's the Mirror Realm?" Lacey asked, a part of her brain still trying to reassure her that this was all some elaborate dream that she wasn't yet ready to wake from. She was still curious enough to want to continue the ride.

"The Mirror Realm, or the Realm of Mirrors, as some call it, is a twin of your world. A *reflection,* if you like."

Glancing between Fletcher and Abe, Lacey said, "Apart from the trees, the sky, and the horses, this doesn't look anything like home."

"The Mirror Realm is your home's *reflection*, but not an exact mirror image," Fletcher explained. "Its *reflection* ripples like a pond that has had a stone thrown into it. Therefore, there are subtle differences."

For the first time since pulling Lacey into the mirror, Abe looked at her and had trouble believing that she could be the Mirror Realm's saviour.

"*Subtle!*" Lacey scoffed in disbelief. "Back home we don't have giant wolves that are really men, and we *definitely* don't have ghostly-things dropping from the trees and sprouting from the ground." She glanced at both Fletcher and Abe before adding, "And I don't want to be rude or anything, but you're kind of way too hairy for regular guys. And you both have the whole pointed ear and sharp teeth thing going on…"

"I get the impression that you're not taking this seriously," Fletcher said, "and that you find this – the Mirror Realm – me and my son, amusing somehow."

"What's to take seriously?" Lacey asked, a wry smile playing across her lips. "I mean, this has got to be some kind of dream, right? The pills my uncle has been force-feeding me has sent my mind a bit screwy. I'll wake up soon, which is kind of a shame, because despite the ghosts and the giant wolves, I'm having fun…"

Hearing Lacey talk, Abe shot a quick look in Marco's direction. Seeing that his friend was still asleep, Abe turned his attention back on Lacey. "Be careful what you say, Lacey Swift. Those *ghosts,* as you like to call them, were once Marco's family and friends."

Rolling her eyes, Lacey shrugged. "Look, I didn't mean to cause any offence, but I'm struggling to play catch-up here. If this isn't my uncle's pills messing with my head, then this is all new to me. I don't have a freaking clue as to what you're talking about, or who you and your friend Marco are. Everything is happening at a million miles an hour. One minute I'm running through the woods and the next thing I know – *bam!* Here I am, on the top of a stagecoach and forced to wear a bunch of clothes…"

"Jeez, you really do talk a lot," Abe cut

over her.

Not liking to be interrupted, Lacey glared at Abe. "I'm just trying to say I didn't mean to offend anyone, that's all."

"No offence taken," Fletcher said. "We do appreciate that you know very little of what's been going on, and we don't have too much time to tell you. But we'll explain as much as we can now and the rest you will learn on your journey."

Although Fletcher couldn't see Lacey, he could picture the young woman by her subtle smell, which was clean and bright. The youthfulness of her voice suggested to Fletcher that both Lacey and his son were about the same age. Perhaps Lacey was just a year or two younger, which would make her nineteen, maybe. Although roughly the same age, Abe seemed older somehow. Lacey smelt and sounded very naïve. But that was to be expected. Fletcher knew that before very long, Lacey – whether she wanted to or not – would lose her naivety. She would soon become an old soul as she learnt of her importance in the Mirror Realm.

Lacey looked at both father and son. "Did I hear you right? Did you just say I had to go on a journey? What journey?"

"The journey to save the Queen of the Mirror Realm, of course," Fletcher said, stroking the wolf that rested beside him on the ground.

"*The Queen – Mirror Realm!?*" Lacey gasped, jumping to her feet and staring at Abe and Fletcher. "I'm not going on any journey to save some queen. I've got to get back home to my sister." She pointed a finger at Abe. "You said that my sister's life is in danger!"

Abe looked at his father then back at Lacey. Through his thick shades, Abe saw everything in hues of yellow, orange, and red – as if the whole world was on fire. Eyeing Lacey, he could see tendrils of colour curling about her like flames.

"Save our Queen and you save your sister – they are one and the same – they are reflections of each other," Abe said.

Closing her eyes and slapping her forehead with the palms of her hands, Lacey said to herself, "Come on, Lacey, wake up! You've got to be dreaming! Wake up!"

"You're not asleep, Lacey Swift," an unfamiliar voice said.

Lacey opened her eyes. Marco had woken and was sitting perched on the edge of the stones. He peered from beneath his hood across the clearing at her. In the flickering glow of the fire, Lacey thought Marco was ridiculously good-looking. He appeared unnaturally handsome. Inhumanly so. *Was he human?* Lacey wondered. She felt suddenly breathless and couldn't fail to notice how her heart had begun to quicken. Marco no longer looked ashen and drawn. The skin covering his face wasn't blistered, waxy, and feverish as before. In the light cast by the fire, Marco looked energised and striking, as if the night had bought him to life somehow. His eyes were black, his jawline firm and square, with a neat dimple in the centre of his chin. His lips looked soft and full in stark contrast to the bristling stubble that covered the lower half of his face.

"I feel as if I'm asleep," Lacey breathed. "I must be dreaming."

Then Marco was standing beside her. Flinching, Lacey was startled at his sudden appearance. Lacey hadn't seen Marco climb from the rock and walk toward her. It was like Marco had just appeared. The only movement Lacey had seen was a flicker of shadows from the corner of her eye.

The closer Marco got, the more beautiful he became. On closer inspection, Lacey thought that Marco had a roughish-look about him that filled her with a sense of wicked delight. Marco's eyes were so perfectly dark, the light from the fire didn't reflect in them. For the first time ever, Lacey felt speechless. She couldn't figure out if she felt so suddenly tongue-tied because of Marco's striking looks, or his sudden materialization beside her.

Marco looked Lacey up and down. *So this is who he had risked his life for,* he pondered. He felt somewhat disappointed. Marco had been expecting a leader of some kind – someone older in appearance and attitude. Lacey looked barely out of her teens and somewhat awkward in her own skin, despite her confidence. But it was nothing more than an illusion she tried to hide behind. He thought she was pretty enough, and he liked the way her leather coat that was buttoned up the front clung tight to her breasts, and how her black leather trousers had moulded themselves to her shapely thighs. But Marco knew that Lacey's prettiness and sensual figure wouldn't be enough to save the Mirror Realm, her sister, nor the Queen.

Marco could see the look of surprise in her eyes as he appeared so suddenly beside her. "Don't be alarmed," he said, his voice low and soft.

Even his voice oozed sex appeal, Lacey thought. What was wrong with this guy? And that was the problem. There was nothing wrong with him. He seemed perfect. Too perfect. *Wait until Thea caught sight of him,* Lacey thought. She wouldn't be able to contain her delight.

"I'm not alarmed," Lacey said, trying to take control of her racing heart, and praying that the sudden flush of heat she felt in her cheeks hadn't been noticed by Marco. She didn't want him to know that it wasn't the closeness of the fire that had made her feel so suddenly hot.

"We know this is a lot for you to absorb," Marco said. "But believe me and my friends when we tell you that this is no dream that you are in, and the only way of saving your sister is by helping us save our Queen. If we manage to save the both of them, we stop our two worlds from *overlapping*."

"But why is this happening?" Lacey asked, glancing away from Marco and back at Abe and Fletcher. She found his stare too intense – like he was reading her somehow.

"As our two worlds are reflections of each other," Marco continued, despite Lacey having looked away from him, "so are our people. Not all of us, just some of us. Not actual reflections – *shadowy* reflections of each other. Some see it as a gift, some as a curse, and others don't even know they have a *reflection*."

"Their proper title is *replicas*," Abe said, much to Lacey's relief. That meant she could continue looking at him, instead of being drawn by Marco's deep stare again. "But they are better known as the *reflections*."

"Lacey, have you ever heard people say that they have just seen someone's double?"

Fletcher asked.

"I guess so," Lacey nodded, a deep furrow of concentration etched across her brow.

"Well they have," Fletcher continued. "They have seen that person's *reflection*, who has stepped through a mirror into your world."

"It can happen the other way, too," Abe interjected. "Reflections from your home can slip through *their* mirror into our world." And he made a zigzagging motion with his hand as if to illustrate them passing through.

"You said that not everyone has a *reflection*," Lacey said. "Do I have a *reflection* in this mirror world or whatever you call it?"

Again, Marco eyed Lacey in the light of the fire. Once more, he looked at how she was dressed in the long, black coat, leather boots and trousers, crossbows, and holsters. The leather sheathe wrapped about her wrist that contained the daggers and knives that were used to slay vampires. Could Lacey really be the one they had been waiting for?

"No, you don't have a reflection in the Mirror Realm," Marco told her.

Hearing this, Lacey wasn't sure whether to feel disappointed or relieved. "How can you be so sure?"

"If you had a *reflection* you wouldn't be dressed like that, unless that's how you carry yourself in your world?" Marco said.

"Of course not," Lacey sighed, glancing down at the unfamiliar clothing she was wearing. "But what has the way I'm dressed got to do with anything?"

Inching closer to the fire, Abe stoked it again with a stick. Sparks twisted up into the night. Glancing up at Lacey, with the glow of the flames dancing in his dark glasses, Abe said, "If you had a *reflection,* you wouldn't have come through as yourself – you would have been slightly different, but as you're the same in your world as you are here suggests you're just the one – a *loner.*"

"But why did you give me these clothes to wear?"

"Because in this world you will become a Venator Noctis," Abe said.

"What's a ven... ter... noc... or whatever it was you said?" Lacey asked, looking down at herself again and straightening the holsters strapped to her thighs.

"The Venator Noctis are Night Hunters," Marco said.

Lacey nodded her head as if she understood, but really she hadn't the faintest idea what Marco was talking about.

As if sensing her confusion, Abe tried to make things clearer for his new friend. "In your world, a Night Hunter would be something like a police officer."

Lacey felt disappointed at hearing this. "What you're telling me is, I've stepped into another world to become a *copper*?"

"It's not something to be taken lightly," Fletcher said, offended by Lacey's remark. "Only those with the purest of hearts and the most accurate of shots were chosen by our Queen to be Night Hunters. All but a few have lost their lives. So mind what you say."

Hearing Fletcher's admiration for the Night Hunters, and once again sensing that her loose tongue had caused offence, Lacey said, "I'm sorry, I didn't mean to offend anyone. The Night Hunters that are still alive... where are they now?"

Despite Lacey's lack of respect when speaking of the Night Hunters, Fletcher could smell that she had a pure heart, one that had yet to be corrupted. *She might well become the Night Hunter she had to*, Fletcher thought to himself.

"The Night Hunters remain scattered," Fletcher said. "But some say that they have now regrouped in the town of Dawn Wall. It's just rumours, but that's what I've heard."

Lacey was worried that she wouldn't live up to the hype of the Night Hunters. She looked at Abe. "You saw me on that stagecoach. I wouldn't say I was a crack-shot, would you?"

Abe didn't answer. He no longer seemed to be interested in the conversation and had moved to the edge of the clearing, where he was sniffing the air.

"You will learn to master the tools of your trade in time," Marco said, glancing down at the knives and blades that covered the leather strap about her wrist.

"What about you? Do you all have *reflections* in my world, or are you *loners* too?" Lacey asked them.

"No," Fletcher said, sniffing at the air and pulling Una close.

"How come?"

"It is only humans that have reflections," Marco said. "Supernatural creatures like me and my friends – vampires and werewolves – don't reflect very well in mirrors."

Lacey stood and pondered everything she had been told by the others. "So you believe my sister, Thea, that her *reflection* is the Queen of your world?"

Marco nodded his head. He was surprised at how little Lacey appeared to know about her family.

"But isn't the Queen supernatural like you?" Lacey asked.

"She is supernatural for sure – she's a

witch – but she is very different from a vampire or werewolf," Marco explained.

Lacey asked her next question with great care, not wishing to offend any of them again. "So how is your Queen dying?"

"Draconia is slowly poisoning her," Marco replied, then shot a glance over his shoulder at Abe.

Abe was standing rigid, as if carved from stone, and continued to sniff at the air.

"Who's Draconia?" Lacey asked.

Marco stared at Lacey again. "He is a sorcerer. Draconia is your uncle's reflection," he said, before vanishing in a flutter of shadows.

Blinking in wonder, Lacey watched as Marco reappeared next to Abe on the other side of the clearing, just as something came snarling out of the darkness toward them.

Chapter Nine

For someone, who as far as Lacey was aware had no sight, Fletcher shot to his feet with surprising grace. Una leapt onto all fours. The wolf's snout curled back to reveal her jagged teeth, and she snarled. Two of the huge wolves that had chased Lacey and Abe across the desert sprang into the clearing in an explosion of broken branches and leaves. They were as big as bears. They threw back their giant heads and released a chorus of throaty howls.

"The Wolf-gatherers have come to hunt us out!" Abe shouted.

"Get back!" Marco warned the others, before flittering away in a spray of shadows to avoid the reach of the howling and snarling wolves.

Lacey stared up at the enormous wolves that now reared up on their back legs in the centre of the clearing. Without thinking, Lacey reached for the crossbows strapped to her leather-clad thighs. Her fingers twitched as she fumbled to release them from their holsters.

Fletcher circled the edge of the clearing, his guide barking and snarling at his side.

Although Fletcher was tall, broad, and muscular, the giant wolves were so big they made him look small and insignificant. Fletcher sniffed the air. He could smell the wolves' anger and hunger for flesh. He couldn't see the creatures, but he knew they were colossal because their scent was strong and suffocating. Since losing his eyes, Fletcher's sense of smell and hearing had become sharper. These senses let him *see* things now.

The black, fur-covered wolves roared with such ferocity that Lacey feared her eardrums would burst. The wolves had long muzzles that, when opened, revealed gums full of teeth standing in jagged rows like knives. Their eyes blazed red as they came forward on their serrated paws toward Lacey and her companions.

"I'll try and shoot them," Lacey said, more to herself than her friends as she fumbled to release the crossbows. Her heart raced, not just because she was terrified at the sight of the wolves, but because of the conversation she had been having with Marco, Abe, and Fletcher. They seemed to believe that she had come to save them, their world, and their Queen. Lacey knew that she had barely been able to save herself and sister from her uncle. But their expectations of her now felt like a heavy weight bearing down upon her. She knew that Abe thought she was too *girlie-fied* to save anyone, and she believed Marco felt the same about her. She had seen the way he had looked her up and down. She had noted the disappointment in his dark eyes.

Marco appeared suddenly at her side. "Hurry, Lacey," he whispered in her ear. "Shoot the wolves and save us."

She glanced at him. Why was it suddenly *her* sole responsibility to kill the wolves? Didn't Marco, Abe, or Fletcher have weapons? Was she being tested by her new friends? Were they waiting to see how she would react in a moment of danger? She felt her hands continue to tremble as she tried to free the crossbows. The giant wolves were closer now. She looked into Marco's dark eyes. "I need some help," she whispered. "I can't kill them on my own."

Marco made no reply. He disappeared from her side in a flutter of black shadows. Marco knew that Lacey wouldn't be able to help them now – if ever. He knew that if they were to stand any chance of killing the wolves, he would have to find a way of drawing their attention so the others could make their attack.

Abe could see that Lacey was having trouble drawing the only weapons that were available to him and his friends. Springing forward, Abe clawed the crossbows from the holsters strapped to Lacey's thighs. He thrust them into her quivering hands. "Now, how about you show us what a great Night Hunter you are." Then he was off again.

To Lacey's amazement, she watched Abe drop onto all fours and bound like a dog toward the wolves. She brought the crossbows up to take aim as the wolves suddenly wheeled round in the centre of the clearing, as if distracted by something. As Lacey peered down the length of the crossbows, she could see what the creatures' attention had been drawn to. A dark shadow was fluttering above their heads. It was like a squall of crows had appeared in the sky above them. It swooped back and forth through the night above the twisting and smoky fire. With the wolves' attention distracted, Fletcher rushed forward, Una at his side. Even though he was blind, Fletcher flung himself into the air, sinking his claw-like hands in the throat of one of the giant wolves. The smell of the blood jetting from the jagged wound was so overpowering, Fletcher guessed that if he still had eyes they would now be streaming.

The wolf reared up on its back legs, using its front paws to swipe and tear at Fletcher. Una shot through the creature's legs and sprang up onto its back. She began to rip chunks of fur and flesh from the wolf. The giant wolf howled. Both

Fletcher and Una clung to the wolf as it tried to shake them free.

"What are you waiting for, Lacey Swift?" Abe shouted. "Shoot!" Then, howling like a wolf himself, he sunk his fangs into the back leg of the second giant wolf. The wolf wailed, its crimson eyes swivelling in their sockets. Abe tightened his jaws.

Steadying her hands, Lacey fought to take aim at the ferocious wolf. But with both wolves now lurching left and right, spinning around and around, her friends kept appearing in her line of fire.

"Hurry, Lacey!" Marco shouted.

Lacey glanced up to see that Marco had reformed. He no longer looked like a fleeting black shadow, and was dropping out of the sky. He struck the wolf that Abe was struggling with. Marco's fingers, which protruded from the ends of his fingerless leather gloves, now looked like claws. Each finger was capped with a razor-sharp fingernail. He raked them down the length of the wolf's back.

"I can't get a clear shot!" Lacey cried, above the bedlam of the wolves' howling and snarling.

"What, they're not big enough for you?" Marco shouted back across the clearing at her.

"Very freaking funny," Lacey hissed under

her breath, closing one eye and pointing the crossbows forward. She aimed the right at the first wolf, the left at the second.

Taking hold of the wolf by the throat, Marco struggled to hold on as it tried to bite and rip at him with its jagged teeth. The second wolf continued to thrash about as Fletcher and Una fought with it.

With her heart lodged in the back of her throat, and eyes nothing more than slits, Lacey steadied her outstretched arms. She squeezed down on the triggers. The wolf lurched around as Fletcher clung to it.

"Hurry, Lacey! I can't hold on for much longer!" Fletcher shouted.

Abe hung to the other wolf's back leg by his jaws as Marco continued to rake his claws over its throat. Sparks flew up into the night like fireflies as the wolf stumbled into the campfire. Then came two loud bangs in quick procession. Lacey opened her eyes. She saw two wispy streams of smoke coiling up from the ends of the crossbows.

Wailing and howling, the giant wolves staggered forward. Lacey could see that each of them had a large gaping wound in the centre of their colossal skulls. Blood streamed from the smoking holes into their eyes, and down the length of their whiskered snouts.

Feeling numb, Lacey watched as the wolves lolloped toward her. Everything seemed to slow, as if time had stopped. The wolves swayed as her friends sprung away. Lacey continued to stand stock-still, staring up at them. The dying wolves approached her, as if their final act would be to kill the person who had shot them. Just as their hot breath caressed her cheeks like a kiss, Marco was sweeping Lacey away in his arms. The freakishly big wolves thundered into the ground, their skulls making a sickening crack as they hit the forest floor. Their huge and blooded bodies came to rest inches from where Lacey was now standing with Marco, his arms wrapped tight about her.

She eased herself away from him. She didn't believe she had needed Marco to save her. Holding the smoking crossbows, Lacey looked at the wolves. Each released a deep, rasping sigh before falling still. Abe and Fletcher, led by Una, joined Lacey and Marco by the wolves. For what seemed like forever, the four of them stood without speaking.

Lacey looked back down at the wolves, but both were now men. Both wore loose-fitting denim shirts and jeans that were stained with blood. And just like Abe and his father, they had thick, dark hair, bushy side whiskers, and pointed ears. Lacey's heart felt like a heavy knot in her chest as she looked down at them. Once again, she felt the unbearable weight of guilt knowing that she had killed what appeared to be two men.

"You did well, Lacey Swift," Fletcher said, breaking the silence.

"Let's get them buried, then perhaps Lacey can catch us some supper," Marco said, stomping on the praise that Fletcher had just offered her.

Holstering her crossbows, Lacey made no reply to Marco's comment. Marco might be a hot-looking vampire – Blood Runner, she thought to herself – but his attitude sucked. Lacey turned her back on him and headed toward the fire.

Chapter Ten

Glancing back over his shoulder, Victor watched his mirror shatter and fall to the floor of the stone corridor in glittering shards of glass. He waited until each piece vanished to nothing more than a sparking pile of dust. The flames from the torches which lined the corridor walls flickered, and for a moment everything went dark. Victor didn't mind the dark, in fact, he preferred it. The corridor began to glow orange and red again as he crept along it, casting long, black shadows behind him as if he had wings.

This wasn't the first time Victor had been through the mirrors and into the realm beyond them. He had visited many times before. The first trip had been by chance many years ago while studying at the Royal College of Medicine in London. He had been working late one night into the small hours, trying to cram for a very important exam he was taking the following day.

Unlike his fellow students, Victor had been left to study alone in the quietness of the college library. Creeping down in the dead of night, he would sit hunched over thick, leather-bound medical journals. His peers had long since gone back to their dormitories. Victor had always struggled to make friends. Even as a boy, he had been bullied and teased about his long legs and gaunt, pale complexion.

"Here comes that freaky ghost!" his classmates had often heckled.

"Here comes spooky-legs! What a freak!" others would shout, as they jeered and mocked him. He hated being called a freak. Always had. Always would. He wasn't a freak, he was just different, that was all. But as he got older, the taunts and name-calling hadn't lessened, they had only got more severe and had come with violence.

The day he realised how alone and truly hated he was, Victor had been on his way home after hunting through thrift stores for second-hand books. He had been sixteen at the time, nearly a man. To prevent himself being chased and jeered, Victor stuck to the narrow backstreets and alleyways. He had reached the halfway point of one such alleyway, when he was struck from behind. He hit the ground with a hard thump, the dog-eared books he had bought spilling from under his arm. He looked up to find himself surrounded by a group of youths who were similar in age to him. Although he didn't know their names, he recognised them. He had often seen them hanging about the town, getting drunk and fighting. He had seen them being thrown into the back of police vans on several occasions, handcuffs about their wrists.

Now this same group, male and female, loomed over him as he crawled about on his hands and knees in the alleyway desperately trying to gather up his books. As he reached for one, his hand was stomped on by a large boot. Pain exploded in his hand, like each of his fingers had received a hammer blow. He felt sick as he cradled his hand to his chest. His long, lank hair fell across his gaunt face. He was struck from behind again. The blow was so hard, the alleyway seesawed before him. Victor hit the ground, blood gushing from his mouth and nose.

"What a fucking freak," someone said.

Victor glanced up to see that he was surrounded. He drew his long legs up to his chest, trying to make himself as small as possible.

He was kicked in the ribs. He was kicked in the back, arms, legs, and head. Knots of pain exploded all over his body as he cried out. Victor didn't want his attackers to know that they were hurting him, but he couldn't stop himself from doing so.

"Get his trousers off," he heard someone screech. "I want to see if his cock is as thin and as pathetic as the rest of him." The voice had been too thin and whining to have come from one of the males. It was a female who had spoken and was now urging the rest of the group to remove Victor's trousers and shorts.

Terrified that he was going to be stripped bare by the savage group, Victor took his hands from over his face and gripped the belt that secured the trousers about his waist. He didn't want them to see him naked. He didn't want them to see how painfully thin he was – how his ribs were clearly visible through his pale flesh. He didn't want them to laugh at his scrawny butt, bony shoulders, knees, and hips. Victor didn't want his private parts exposed to be mocked and laughed at. He doubted he would be strong enough to ever get over such a degrading experience. It would haunt him for the rest of his life. Strip him of the little masculinity he felt.

Hands grabbed his trousers. He felt them being tugged down. "Please don't," he cried out. "Please stop." He gripped his trousers about the waist and kicked out with his legs, trying to shake free the hands that were mauling him.

"Hold him still, for fuck's sake," he heard one of them shout. It was the girl's voice he had heard before. "Pin him down. I want to see how small his dick is."

Terrified beyond belief, Victor looked up into the face of the girl who was goading the rest of the group on. They tore at his clothes like a pack of wild animals. Victor looked up into her face. He searched her eyes, hoping that he might see some spark of humanity in them. "Please – I beg you – please..."

The girl leered down at him. Her eyes were red-rimmed and glazed as if high on some drug, or maybe she was drunk. Victor knew that there would be no reasoning with her.

"Shhh," she said, as the males in the group pinned his arms and legs to the ground. "I just want to take a peek," the girl grinned, unbuckling his trouser belt. Her eyes never left Victor's as she worked his trousers and shorts down. "What am I going to find?" she teased, her lips twisting up into a cruel smile. She glanced down at his flaccid penis and began to laugh.

Victor closed his eyes. He couldn't bear it. He couldn't bear being exposed and mocked like this. He had never known such humiliation. He felt an agonising pain splinter through him like an ice-cold poker as the girl gripped him in her hand. The pain was so intense that he was forced to open his eyes as they bulged in their sockets. Through his tears and pain, he scanned the jeering faces of the group. One of them must take pity on him – help him. Amongst the sea of faces, he saw one that he did recognise. He saw the face of his twelve-year-old brother, Edward. He was standing behind the group, not with them. He had heard the commotion as he'd happened to pass the entrance to the alley, and had come to investigate. He now wished that he hadn't. Victor could see that just like his own, Edward's face was covered with tears. He looked shocked and confused, but most of all frightened at seeing his older brother treated in such a cruel way.

Victor stared at his younger brother and their eyes locked. In them, Victor could see fear and his brother's shame. It was that look of shame which hurt Victor the most. It wasn't the kicks and the punches, or the pain in his groin – it was the look of embarrassment in his younger brother's eyes that hurt the most.

Wasn't an older brother meant to be stronger and more powerful – the protector and role model? Yet here *he* was, his trousers pulled down to his knees, humiliated and demoralised by the gang of youths that had attacked him. Victor glared up at his tormentors. He stared up through his tears and he hated them. He hated all of them. But most of all, he hated Edward for looking at him in that way. He hated Edward for seeing him like this.

Then they stopped. His persecutors had either grown tired or bored with their attack, but whichever it was they let go of his limbs. The girl climbed from him, a knowing smile across her face. They sauntered back down the alley whooping and laughing as they went. Just one stayed, his perfectly round face smeared with tears.

"I hate you!" Victor hissed, pulling up his shorts and trousers. He staggered to his feet, the pain in his groin knifing into the pit of his stomach. "Stop looking at me like that!" he screeched at Edward, spit flying from his lips.

Watching his older brother straighten his clothes, Edward continued to sob.

"I'll show you!" Victor screeched. "I'll show *all* of you that I'm not the fucking weakling you think I am. One day I'll be more powerful than you could ever believe!"

Edward just stood and sniffed, confused that his big brother, Victor, could hate him. After all, he hadn't called Victor names. He hadn't kicked and punched him – pulled down his trousers. Edward had just wanted to help, but was too small compared to the others.

Snatching up his books and looking back at Edward, Victor said just above a whisper, "If you want spooky, I'll show you fucking *spooky!*" He then limped away, one hand placed flat against his stomach.

If Victor had been a loner before, he became a complete recluse after this incident. Spending hours locked away in his bedroom with his head buried between the pages of science manuals. There were also the books he kept hidden away under the mattress and in a secret shoebox at the back of his wardrobe. These were the books he didn't want anyone to see – the books that spoke of dark things. These were the books that taught the secrets of the *Demonic Arts*. They had titles like, *'The Eternal Wisdom'*, *'The Satanic Formula'*, and *'The Spirit Guide'*. Each of these books had been bound in a black, leathery-type material that felt cold and waxen to the touch – like the skin of a corpse.

Victor hadn't ordered these through the library. He hadn't come across them buried beneath piles of yellow-stained newspapers in the second-hand bookshops he frequented. They had been left just outside his bedroom door, stacked in neat little bundles and tied together with tangled lengths of human hair. Victor had no idea who had left these for him and why, and he wouldn't find out for several more years. Not until he was studying alone one night to be a doctor, bent over his medical books in the quiet of the college library.

The bang had been so sudden and violent that Victor had jumped from his seat, scattering his revision notes into the air. He watched as they see-sawed to the library floor. Bending at the waist, he reached over with his long arms and gathered his notes together. His handwriting was messy and readable only to him. The words were written in black ink that spiralled and looped across the pages, as if a spider had dipped its feet in an inkwell and then raced across his work.

Gathering the last of the pages together, Victor heard another bang. This time it was quieter and was followed by another and then another. Placing his work on the table he called out, "Hello? Is anybody there?"

He waited in the stillness of the library, but there was no answer apart from the constant banging. Creeping around the edge of the table, Victor followed the sound. It seemed to be coming from between two rows of shelves that were crammed with books from top to bottom. Making his way toward the end of the row of books, Victor peered down the aisle. Narrowing his dark, beady eyes, he looked with curiosity at the mirror which stood in the middle of the aisle between the two rows of bookshelves.

The mirror didn't seem to be attached to anything. There was no frame or fitting, yet it stood erect in the centre of the aisle. He could see his reflection in it. Tall, dark, and thin. Victor glanced back over his shoulder at the table where he had been working moments ago. He could see his paperwork scattered across the table beneath the glow of the lamp.

"Hello?" Victor called out again. "If this is some kind of joke then I'm not laughing." Again, he was met by silence, other than the continuous banging sound that seemed to be coming from the mirror. Victor turned back to face it. Without further hesitation, he walked toward the mirror as his reflection walked toward him. As they drew nearer to each other, his reflection began to change shape. It was as if his reflection was beginning to ripple and warp out of shape and take on a new one. Still wondering if this wasn't some cruel prank being played on him, Victor glanced once more back over his shoulder and into the library. But he could see no one. He faced the mirror once more. He staggered away from it, throwing his thin, pale hands to his narrow face.

On the other side of the mirror stood a shrouded figure. The cloth that covered this figure from head to toe looked thin and almost lucid. It twitched and shifted in the wind that howled on the other side of the mirror. The figure was as tall and as awkward-looking as Victor himself. Its face was masked by a hood that was draped over the stranger's head and shoulders.

"Who are you?" Victor asked.

Without answering, the figure raised one knotted finger. "Shhh," he whispered. The sound was deep and rasping.

Peering over the figure's shoulder, Victor could see that whatever strange world lay on the other side of the mirror, it was night there. The dark sky suddenly flashed with streaks of blue and pink lightning. The sound of thunder followed, and Victor realised this had been the banging sound he had heard. Far off in the distance, Victor could see a tower that reached so far into the sky, he lost sight of its peak amongst the dark, rolling clouds.

"Who are you?" he asked the figure again.

This time, the figure responded by pulling back its hood. Victor wanted to take another step backwards, but his lanky legs wouldn't move. It was like someone had crept up and nailed his shoes to the library floor.

The figure's hood fell about its shoulders. Victor looked into the face that had been revealed on the other side of the mirror. At first he thought he was looking at some distorted reflection of himself as the person staring back at him looked so much like him. The stranger looked so similar in appearance to Victor that he could have been his brother. But the stranger's face was ravaged with age. The skin that covered his skull was barely there – faded and wizened – knotted into thick wrinkles. Where there had once been eyes were now two dark pits. The mouth was just a bloodless slit.

The figure held out one twisted hand. Now fascinated rather than scared, Victor took hold of it and stepped into the mirror.

"Did you enjoy the books?" the figure asked in a voice so deep and rasping, it sounded as if he were being strangled.

Victor smiled to himself as he recalled that first meeting all those years ago, and at everything he had been shown and taught since. Reaching the end of the corridor, Victor turned right. He knew the tower so well by now, he felt he could navigate it blindfolded. Little had he known all those years ago, when he had first seen it in that mirror, that it would become a sanctuary for him. A place where he could be himself, practice his medicine, and someday soon become a king. He felt at peace in the Splinter.

Reaching the end of the corridor, Victor climbed a set of stone stairs that corkscrewed their way up into darkness. At the top was a door which led into a long, circular room. It was lit with a series of candles attached to long metal rods that protruded from the floor like spikes. At the far end there was a high-backed throne that reached almost to the pointed ceiling. Its legs were twisted like the roots of a tree, and the arms coiled upwards like rotten branches. On the throne sat a shrouded figure who was slumped forward as if asleep.

Victor stopped before the throne and the figure that sat upon it.

"You have been careless, my friend," the figure croaked without moving from his slumped position in the enormous throne.

Victor's jet-black eyes darted back and forth in their sockets, racking his brain in search of what the figure could mean. "Careless, Draconia? I'm not sure..."

"Where is your niece, Lacey Swift?" Draconia asked, his voice sounding torn and dry.

"Well, she's – um..." Victor mumbled, wringing his hands anxiously together.

"She's *here!*" Draconia roared, without looking up – without moving. "She's come into the Mirror Realm."

"Are you sure?" Victor said, startled by this piece of news. He knew she had escaped, but into the woods, not here. "But how?"

"Through a mirror, of course."

"But how?" was all Victor could muster again, as his head began to ache with a dull thud behind his eyes.

"The longer it takes for us to find the key to the box, there is a risk that more mirrors will begin to appear. More mirrors, more people who could hinder our plan," Draconia seethed from beneath his shroud.

"But Lacey is nothing. Insignificant!" Victor tried to reassure him.

"She could complicate matters," Draconia rasped, unmoved upon his throne.

"She's nothing and I will deal with her when she returns," Victor said.

As if being pulled by invisible strings, Draconia raised his head. From beneath his shifting robes, he stared at Victor.

"I've received word from the Wolf-gatherers that your niece was dressed in the uniform of a *Night Hunter*. They said she was protected by a Blood Runner. Perhaps we have both underestimated her *significance* in our plan."

"Nonsense, my dear friend," Victor said. "Lacey is nothing and has come to this land by chance. On her return to my world, I will make sure that she causes us no further problems."

Draconia then made a deep, gasping sound and Victor wasn't sure if he was trying to cough or laugh.

"Victor, she will never return to your world. I have made sure of that. I have released the Guardians to deal with her."

Hearing this, Victor couldn't help but shudder as he pictured the Guardians with their swordsticks, their white mercury venom, and their devastating solar energies. Draconia sensed Victor's fear.

"You're not softening, are you?" Draconia asked.

"No, of course not, my friend, but... the Guardians..."

Grinning beneath his hood, Draconia changed the subject. "Enough of your niece, she will be dealt with as were her parents. But what about her sister, Thea?"

"It will just be a day or two now before she is in a total catatonic state," Victor grinned along with his reflection.

"Good, good. Excellent," Draconia whispered. "The Queen is near death. It is important that we get this right, Victor. They have to die at the exact same moment."

"Why don't we just kill them now? Both of them together?" Victor asked. The thought of killing Thea and the Queen excited him.

"The Queen will only die the moment I have the piece of mirror from the box. It will be at that moment I become whole again. I will then be strong enough to kill the Queen, and at that moment, you can kill Thea."

"Let me bring Thea through the mirrors – to the Splinter. It would be..." Victor started.

"No! No! No!" Draconia gagged. "Thea is not to be brought here. The Queen and your niece will grow stronger if they come together. They have to be kept apart."

"But..." Victor said.

"No buts, Victor. Now go back through your mirror and watch the girl. Leave Lacey to me," Draconia said, lowering his head and dismissing his reflection.

Chapter Eleven

Marco and Abe stepped into the clearing, two dead rabbits swinging from their fists. Using their claws like tools, they cut away the rabbits' skins and tore off strips of pink meat. Lacey and her new companions sat by the fire. The temperature had dropped and they warmed themselves before the flames.

Stealing the odd glance, Lacey looked at Marco who sat beside her. Despite thinking that he truly was beautiful, she thought that perhaps he had an arrogance she did not like or could warm to. Didn't he – didn't any of them – understand that shooting crossbows and killing was alien to her? It wasn't something she enjoyed or wanted to do. Despite those men being giant wolves, she now felt guilty for killing them. Once dead, they looked too human – too much like her. She had never killed so much as a fly, but was now expected to kill at will – on her companions' say so. It was fast dawning on Lacey that she wasn't in a dream nor a nightmare that she would wake from. Wouldn't she have done so by now?

Marco glanced at Lacey and she looked

away. She didn't want Marco to know that she found it difficult not to look at him.

Remembering how Abe had told her that Marco was related to those ghost-like creatures, Lacey had trouble believing that he could be one of them. Stealing another glance, she watched how the flames illuminated Marco's pale face, and gave his dark hair the appearance of molten lava.

"Why do you keep looking at me?" Marco asked without looking at her.

Because you're gorgeous, despite your dominating attitude, she wanted to say. But didn't. She still had some self-respect despite now considering herself a killer. "I just find it hard to believe that you could be related to... those..."

"*Things?*" Marco cut in.

"Well... yeah... I guess."

Marco turned his dark eyes on her. "Like me, they were once Blood Runners. But I am their sole survivor."

"What happened to your people?" Lacey asked, not knowing how far to push the subject with him for fear of causing offence again.

Marco looked toward the fire, face now looking drawn, as if in pain. "Draconia's armies murdered them."

"But why?"

"Draconia knew that my people had

certain unique powers that no other species of vampire has. He knew that we could *blink* and - "

"What's *blink?*" Lacey asked, leaning closer to the fire, as the temperature continued to drop.

"You might have noticed that I don't stay in the same place for too long. One minute I'm there and the next second I'm gone and can reappear some distance away. Well that's what we call '*blinking*' – in the *blink* of an eye I am gone," Marco explained, *blinking* away and reappearing on the opposite side of the campfire as if to illustrate the point to Lacey.

"But why would this sorcerer – Draconia – destroy your people because you can *blink*?" Lacey asked as Abe and Fletcher finished cutting meat from the rabbit carcasses with their claw-like hands.

"Because Draconia wants to rule the Mirror Realm," Fletcher said, letting Una lick the rabbit's blood from his fingers. "Draconia hoped that he could persuade the Blood Runners to join him in his quest to overthrow the Queen and her army of Night Hunters."

Abe placed the rabbit meat on the ground in thin, pink strips. He passed one to his father, skewered another two pieces onto a pointed stick, and then passed one each to Marco and Lacey.

Abe looked at Lacey as she took the skewer from him. "You'll probably prefer yours cooked," he said.

Lacey looked down at the bloody piece of meat she had been handed. Glancing across the clearing at Marco, she could see that he was already gnawing at the rabbit meat. Noticing Lacey's look of revulsion, he half smiled and said, "You don't want to kill and won't eat raw meat; what exactly do you do?"

Trying her very best to ignore him, Lacey dangled the skewered meat over the fire. She glanced through the flames at Abe and Fletcher, who were both shoving the uncooked meat into their mouths. Abe released a belch that rattled through the air.

Grinning at the disgusted look on Lacey's face, Abe said, "Excuse me, but it tastes so damn good!"

Fletcher turned the conversation back to Draconia. "The sorcerer had hoped that the Blood Runners would join him and he would be able to use their unique *blinking* abilities to defeat the Night Hunters."

"Why did he want your people to join him?" Lacey asked Marco, turning the meat over the fire.

"What an army we would've made," Marco said, his dark eyes haunted. "Imagine an army that could *blink* across a battlefield, never being in the same place long enough for the Night Hunters to take aim. To be able to change battle formation in the *blink* of an eye. To surround them in an instance. We would've been invincible."

"So a meeting was called in the vast banqueting halls of the Splinter by Draconia for all of the Blood Runners to attend," Fletcher said, pulling small pieces of the raw meat apart, rolling them between his thick thumb and forefinger and feeding them to Una, who lay curled at his side.

"The Splinter?" Lacey asked. "What's the Splinter?"

"The Queen's tower and the axis to all mirrors," Fletcher began to explain. "The Mirror Realm spins around it, as does your world, and some say other worlds or layers, too."

Marco licked the rabbit's blood from his fingers, then said, "But when my father, the leader of my people, refused to join him, Draconia smiled and told them to leave the Splinter in peace. But Draconia was keeping a secret. He had cursed my people with one of his many demonic spells. As my people were unwilling to use their abilities to *blink* to help Draconia overthrow the Queen and her army of Night Hunters, he took their gift to *blink* away."

Picking up another slither of bloody meat, Marco ripped it into chunks then popped it into his mouth. As he chewed the meat he continued, "It wasn't until my people stepped from the Splinter into the burning glare of the desert to find that their stagecoaches had been taken that they realised they had been deceived. Their skin began to itch in the heat of the sun and they knew they had to get back to the safety of the Sleeping Caves, which used to be our home. The caves were four nights' travel away and, as they could *blink* just short distances at a time, my people knew they would never reach the safety of the caves without being burnt alive." Marco placed another piece of meat into his mouth and chewed.

Wiping blood from his lips with the back of his hand, Abe said, "The Blood Runners' only chance of survival was to *blink* across the desert to these forests. The trees would have shielded them from the searing heat of the desert sun. But as they tried to *blink* they realised they couldn't. Their gift had been taken away from them."

"So my father, with his skin peeling and blistering," Marco said, "led his people across the desert and to the Howling Forests. For two days and nights they crawled on their hands and knees, their bodies smouldering and burning in the heat until they reached the safety and shelter of the forest."

"How come they didn't die? How come they have remained like ghosts in this forest?" Lacey asked, pulling her skewered meat from above the fire.

"Draconia won't let them die, not fully," Marco said, his voice dropping to little more than a whisper. "My father and the rest of my people will spend the rest of eternity somewhere between life and death – between the mirrors. They will forever protect these forests and the Moon Howlers who live within them. They remain like... what is it you called them?" He looked across the flames at Lacey. "Ah yes... I remember now... *ghost-things.*"

Lacey cringed now that she understood why her earlier comments had proved so insensitive to Marco. She broke his stare and looked down at the meat. It was overcooked and burnt in places, but even so, her stomach somersaulted at the sight of food. She couldn't remember how long ago it had been since she had last eaten. Lacey guessed that it must have been the dry piece of toast her uncle had given to her before she had escaped him. How long ago was that now? Was it minutes? Hours? She couldn't be sure. Lacey knew she couldn't be sure of anything anymore.

Then a thought came to her. She looked at

Marco. "How come you didn't end up like the rest of your people?" She placed a piece of the burnt rabbit meat into her mouth. It was crispy and dry, but her stomach welcomed it.

"The day my father led my people to the meeting at the Splinter, I had come down with a fever. I had been a child. My father had been reluctant to take me, but my mother hadn't wanted to leave me in the caves unwell on my own. So they made a compromise. I would travel as far as the Howling Forests with them, where I would be left in the charge of Fletcher and his family until my parents returned."

Lacey placed another chunk of meat into her mouth. She swallowed it down. Looking at Fletcher and Abe, she said, "Where are the rest of your people – the Moon Howlers?"

Father and son looked at each other, then at Lacey.

"They left two days ago and are heading for the Snowstorm Mountains. They'll be waiting for us there," Abe said.

"Why didn't you go with them?" Lacey asked.

"We were waiting for you," Fletcher answered. "It was unsafe for our people to stay here any longer. Draconia's dark sorcery is eating away our world, turning it into a wasteland. That desert beyond this forest was once half the size it is now, but day by day, it grows. It stretches, reaching out and taking more of our home. Soon there will be nothing left of the Howling Forests. If we stayed, the desert would take us with it."

"But isn't there any way of stopping it? Of stopping Draconia?" Lacey asked, throwing the leftovers of her supper onto the ground. Seeing this, Una sprang from Fletcher's side, pounced on the food, and began to snuffle it up.

"If we are to save our world, we have to save the Queen and her *reflection* – your sister," Fletcher said.

Wanting nothing more than to save her twin sister, Lacey got to her feet. Placing her hands on the hilts of the crossbows, she said, "Well? What are we waiting for? Let's get going!"

Marco began to chuckle.

Having had enough of his bombastic attitude toward her, Lacey glared at him. "What's so funny?"

Marco continued to grin. "You are."

"Piss off," Lacey said. "I don't see how me wanting to save my sister is so funny. After all, it's you who says that if we save Thea, we save your Queen."

"It's not as easy as that," Fletcher said in his deep voice. "The Queen can only be saved by opening the box that contains one of the Clicks."

"You've lost me," Lacey said with a shake of her head. "What's a click?"

"A sliver of broken glass – a piece of mirror that holds the power to save the Queen and your sister," Fletcher explained.

"So where is the box that contains this piece of broken mirror?" Lacey asked.

"Far away from here," Abe said.

"Shouldn't we get going then?"

"First, we will need to get the key that will open the box," Marco added.

"Where is the key?" Lacey asked, her sole aim now to save her sister.

Abe glanced at his father, then at Lacey. "The prisoner has it."

"And where's this prisoner?" Lacey asked, her mind starting to spin as she tried to make sense of what Abe and the others were telling her.

"He's being held in Bleakstorm Prison on the other side of the Onyx Sea," Abe said, sounding full of dread.

"I guess from the sound of your voice that this is somewhere we really don't want to be going," Lacey said, her hands settling over her crossbows.

Abe stared at her from behind his thick shades. "The Onyx Sea is patrolled by the Angelsharks. A murderous race of immortal slave traders. They can't be bargained nor reasoned with. Some say they can't be killed, as they are dead already. They are believed to be soulless."

"And even if we were to make it safely across the Onyx Sea," Marco cut in, "Bleakstorm Prison is a maze of tunnels that stretch for miles, each one filled with the most evil of killers."

"You're not selling this to me," Lacey said, slumping to the ground, fearing that the rescue of her sister and the Queen was doomed before it had even started. "It sounds impossible," she said looking at them.

"And it well might be," Fletcher said, "but you leave tonight. The dawn is drawing close. Today you shall rest, as you will need every ounce of cunning and energy to survive the journey you are about to make."

"What's this *you* business?" Lacey asked, looking straight at Fletcher. "Aren't you coming with us?"

"I'm sorry, but my blindness will hamper your mission. I will take a separate path from you, head to the Snowstorm Mountains and protect my family and people the best I can."

Lacey looked at Abe, then back at Fletcher. "But what about Abe? He's your son. Isn't he family, too?"

Fletcher bowed his head and spoke in a

voice so low Lacey struggled to hear him. "This is my son's punishment. He has to go with you to make peace with the rest of his family and the Mirror Realm."

Just like his father had moments before, Abe lowered his head as if in shame.

"What could your son have done that was so bad that to earn your forgiveness he has to go on such a dangerous journey?" Lacey asked Fletcher.

He raised his head, the dark, vacant sockets where he'd once had eyes, black with shadow. "Abraham will tell you if he chooses to. Now it is time for you to rest." Without another word Fletcher got to his feet and headed into the forest, Una at his side.

Lacey, Abe, and Marco sat in silence until it became unbearable.

"So why are you putting yourself forward to come on this journey?" Lacey asked Marco, breaking the silence.

Fluttering like shadows in candlelight, Marco *blinked* and reappeared curled on his side by the burning embers of the fire. He lay and looked at Lacey with dark and soulless eyes. "To avenge Draconia for what he did to my people." Closing his eyes, Marco pulled his hood over his head and wrapped his long, dark coat about him, disappearing beneath it.

Rolling onto her back near to the fire, Lacey looked across the clearing at Abe, who continued to sit by the fire, his head hung so low that his chin touched his chest.

What could he have done that was so bad, he would be sent to his almost certain death by his own father? Lacey wondered. With that thought at the forefront of her mind, she slipped into unconsciousness and fell asleep.

Chapter Twelve

Stepping through from the Mirror Realm, and back into his own world, Victor teetered on the edge of the cliff. He pin-wheeled his arms like a tightrope-walker to stop himself falling into the crashing waves below.

"Dammit!" he hissed under his breath.

The mirror shattered behind him before disappearing on the wind like a wave of sparkling dust. Turning away from the cliff edge, Victor saw his cottage in the distance beneath a sky that looked the colour of bruised and battered skin. Morning was minutes away, and by the look of the clouds racing in from the west, he could sense that they were bringing more snow with them.

Regaining his composure, he set off across snow-laden fields to his home and his niece who lay in the upstairs bedroom. She would soon need her morning dose of medicine, and he grinned to himself, that feeling of excitement making his heart quicken. But what he didn't find so funny or exciting was how the mirror he had stepped through had materialized just inches from the cliff-edge. A fraction further in the wrong direction and he would have fallen to his death.

Victor could remember a time when the mirrors stayed still. He could always be certain of stepping through his mirror at the very same point that he had left it. But not now. Something seemed to be changing – *shifting*. The mirrors no longer stayed still and this worried him. What if he stepped through the mirror onto a busy motorway or a railway track with a high-speed passenger train bearing down on him? He knew he would be dead. Victor didn't intend to find out, and the thought caused gooseflesh to crawl up his back.

Victor suspected it had something to do with the sliver of glass in the box. Ever since his *reflection* had moved it from the Splinter, everything had started to change. The two worlds no longer seemed to be running parallel to each other. Now they seemed to be *overlapping*. He had always known that the two worlds had time differences. For instance, he knew that whilst he was fifty-two years old, Draconia, his reflection, seemed to be much older – as if he had been alive for many years. Perhaps hundreds of years. People from the Mirror Realm seemed to live far longer than their *reflections*, but to think about it made his head ache, and he considered himself to be intelligent, far superior to anybody else he knew. The fact that he couldn't quite work out the math frustrated and angered him, so he tried not to think about it, if possible.

Reaching the cottage, he kicked snow from his shoes, then went inside. The first milky-grey rays of morning light seeped through the kitchen windows and onto the table where he prepared Thea's medicine. He knew that he would only have to prepare one dose this morning. One dose from now on, as Draconia's Guardians would soon deal with Lacey, if they hadn't done so already. Victor filled a glass with water, then took one of the black pills from a piece of muslin cloth they were wrapped in. He counted their number and nodded to himself in approval.

"Good, good," he sighed. "I should have enough." He was now glad that he had purchased so many of the poisonous pills from Araghney Ursa, the witch who lived on the outskirts of Rogue Drift, a deserted town in the Mirror Realm. He recalled his journey across the wastelands to seek out the ancient witch. She specialised in concocting the most vile and repugnant of potions and medicines. Victor was meant to have stayed with her for a day or two, but ended up staying for six months, as she was willing to share her demonic-magic with him.

But magic wasn't the only thing they had shared. He had stayed for another reason.

Victor found Araghney Ursa to be putrid-looking and she stank so much of rotting flesh and decay that, for the first month or two, he had worn a handkerchief tied about the lower part of his face whenever she was near to him. But despite her decaying face and flesh, and the rancid smell that emanated from her, Araghney had somehow bewitched him. The sight of her grey, withered, and rotting flesh had made him want to vomit at first, but as the days rolled into weeks and then into months, he had somehow grown fond of her. He had grown to want her.

It had been subtle at first; just the odd flutter of his heart as she got near to him. Then those minor flutterings grew stronger and his heart began to race in his chest every time he had looked at her. Even her revolting smell didn't seem so bad, and he removed the handkerchief from about his face.

Then, one black evening, sitting next to the witch in her shack, Victor had the sudden urge to entwine his fingers amongst the wispy strands of her greasy hair and kiss her cracked and blistered lips. As he drew closer to her, his mouth hovering over hers, Araghney had snatched up a looking-glass. She asked Victor to look at her reflection. And as he peered over her shoulder and into the mirror, he didn't see an old wench looking back, but a beautiful young woman, with thick, luxurious black hair, skin that was blemish-free, perfect blue eyes, and lips that looked full, ripe, and soft. Slowly, Araghney set down the looking-glass. She stood before Victor. And when he looked at her, all he could see was the beautiful young woman he had seen in the mirror. Very slowly, she peeled off her dress revealing a body that any man would trade his soul for just to spend one moment pressed naked against it.

As Victor began to stiffen in his lap, Araghney held out one slender and youthful hand. She closed it around Victor's and led him across the shack to her bed. There, he had sex for the first time. And his heart raced with delight. He had at last found a woman who wanted him for who he was and however he looked. Araghney didn't laugh at his size. Araghney didn't sneer at his penis, but cried out in pleasure as she pulled him into her. He couldn't believe that such a beautiful woman could want him so. But the longer he spent with her, the more depraved and unnatural their lovemaking became. Victor felt as if a darkness had fallen over him. A darkness that seeped into every one of his pores and smothered the last remaining embers of his humanity. During those long days and nights he had spent in Araghney's bed, Victor sensed that any decency he might have once had, had finally been snuffed out. What Araghney had taught him – had shown him – what he had been willing to do and have done to him – was nothing short of depraved.

When he woke one morning several weeks later, thinner and weaker than he had ever felt before, he looked at the woman who lay naked asleep on the bed beside him. But she no longer looked in her mid-twenties, but ancient and old. Her breasts were no longer firm and proud, but lay wrinkled and flat against her rotting flesh. Victor knew that it was time for him to leave. If he didn't leave Araghney, the spell that she had worked on him may never be broken, and he would have stayed with her forever.

And now, as he stood in his kitchen and counted out the remaining pills, he felt relief that he had taken enough of them from Araghney. Victor knew he would never be able to return to her little broken down shack, because if he did, he would never leave. Even as he thought of Araghney now, his heart began to flutter again and there was a small part of him that felt excited at the memories of her.

Picking up the tray, Victor made his way up the stairs to Thea's bedroom. He eased the door open and crept inside. He stalked across the room on his long, thin legs. His shadow spilt over the sleeping girl like a giant claw.

Placing the tray on the bedside cabinet, Victor placed his lips to Thea's ear and whispered, "It's time for your medicine."

Thea stirred, and without opening her eyes, she mumbled, "I... I... don't want any more."

"Of course you do," he soothed. "Your Uncle Victor knows what's best for you."

He then plucked up the pill from the tray. With a hooked forefinger, he pulled down on Thea's lower lip and pushed the pill into her mouth. At once, she began to twist and turn like a snake beneath the bedclothes. He wrapped a hand around her jaw to keep her mouth shut.

"Be a good girl and swallow," he whispered.

Thea tossed to and fro but she was too weak, too tired, to resist him. The pill made its way to the back of her throat. He watched her blue eyes bulge. Victor reached for the glass of water. Parting her lips just a fraction, he poured some of it in.

Thea made an involuntary gurgling sound in the back of her throat and spluttered, causing some of the water to seep from the corners of her mouth. Snapping her jaws closed, Victor screeched, "Swallow, you little bitch. *Swallow!*"

He watched as Thea's windpipe almost popped from her neck as she forced the pill down. She became still again.

Victor smiled. "Good girl." He drew his fingers furtively over her feverish brow. Once he was sure she was asleep once more, Victor crept from her room. He took the tray back to the kitchen, where he turned his thoughts to Lacey.

Chapter Thirteen

While Abe, Marco, and Lacey slept, Fletcher spent the day in the Howling Forests gathering together supplies for the journey that lay ahead for his son and his friends. Using his acute sense of smell, Fletcher and Una hunted down some more rabbits. With his hook-like fingers, Fletcher blindly skinned them, wrapping large chunks of its flesh up in leaves to be kept moist and fresh. He placed the wraps of meat into his trouser pockets and the remaining parcels he stuffed inside his shirt.

Using Una as his guide, Fletcher made his way down to the river where he filled three drinking bottles made from deer hide. The previous day, he had left three woven holdalls on the river bank. One each for Abe and his friends. Fletcher had also concealed Abe's bow and Marco's sword and slingshot. He knew he had taken a risk by not letting Abe and Marco take their weapons out into the desert with them, but he had wanted to see if Lacey Swift was not only capable of defending herself, but also saving Abe and Marco if she needed to. She had been hesitant when the Wolf-gatherers had attacked, but she had shot them eventually, despite knowing that they became men once more when they were dead. He understood the difficulty she faced in doing so, but if she was going to survive in the Mirror Realm – if Lacey was going to save her sister and the Queen – she would have to quickly learn to put aside any fears of misgivings that she might have. This was a whole new world – a world that Lacey was going to have to come quickly accustomed to – or die.

Once Fletcher had finished scavenging with his shrewd sense of smell for fruit and berries that Lacey and the others could take with them on their journey, he placed them into the holdalls and headed deeper into the forest, Una constantly at his side. Fletcher knew that Lacey would be able to use her crossbows, which had once been blessed by the Queen, giving it her grace and power so that it would never need to be reloaded and forever fire an everlasting supply of arrows. But his son Abe and his friend Marco didn't have the enchanted weapons of a Night Hunter. He knew that Abe would need arrows, and lots of them, if he was going to survive the journey he had to make. Fletcher was no witch like the Queen, but he did know of something that was very powerful – yet if not used with care and caution, could be very dangerous.

"Take me to the biggest and ripest inferno-bush you can find," Fletcher commanded Una.

Sniffing at the air with her long, whiskered snout, Una made her way through the forest, Fletcher at her side. As he let the wolf lead him, Fletcher remembered how, as a boy and before he had been blinded, he and his friends had taken the berries from the inferno bush and had played the game *'Blast'* with them. Smiling to himself, Fletcher pictured him and his friends catapulting the inferno berries at each other as they charged through the Howling Forests. If hit by one of the charcoal-looking berries, it would blast open on impact and sting you like a wasp. The pain it unleashed hadn't been agony, just uncomfortable as it sent a burning sensation through the body. It didn't last long, just enough to stun you and make you wail.

However, it had been by chance one evening at the end of a hike through the Howling Forests that Fletcher had learnt the true ferocity of the inferno berries. Noah, who had been his best friend, had by accident dropped some into their campfire. They watched as the berries had grown hot in the fire, then hissed and spat until they exploded in a hideous ball of blue flames.

Fletcher and Noah had both been thrown backwards through the air under the force of the blast, and landed some distance away. They looked at one another as they lay slumped at the foot of a tree.

"Whoa!" Noah had said, smiling from ear-to-ear.

"What was that?" Fletcher asked dazed and confused.

"It was those berries. No wonder they're called inferno berries," Noah said, his face breaking into a grin.

"I won't be messing with them again," Fletcher said, pulling lumps of singed hair from his head.

"What do you mean?" Noah said. "Think of the fun we could have with them. Maybe we could heat them up just enough so they don't explode. Who knows what would happen then."

"That's what frightens me!" Fletcher called after his friend, who had disappeared into the undergrowth in search of the nearest inferno bush.

Fletcher wasn't so sure that he should help Noah find any more of the berries. Noah wasn't very much liked by the rest of the Moon Howlers. They saw the boy as being somewhat odd – different from the rest of them. No one quite knew who Noah's parents were or where, in fact, he had come from. He had been found one day by the Elders, strolling in the forest. They had brought Noah back to the village believing he was a lost child. So Noah stayed. Some of Fletcher's people wished he had not been found and not stayed. They claimed that the boy's face could change. Some said that sometimes when they looked at him – caught a fleeting glimpse of him – that the boy's face looked different – *unfamiliar*. They said that he looked like a completely different boy altogether. Some weren't sure whether Noah was a wolf, vampire, or some other supernatural creature altogether. But when they looked again, Noah was once more like he always had been. Fletcher had often wondered if such claims were nothing more than exaggerations, because Noah had always looked the same to him. But there weren't many of his people who liked the boy. Fletcher liked him, though – perhaps more out of pity than true friendship. He didn't like the idea of someone being left out – *pushed* away.

So they sat for the rest of the afternoon until it grew dark, experimenting with the berries. They heated them and then reheated them, but were careful not to let them touch the flames of their campfire.

Fletcher and Noah let them cool on the forest floor. As soon as they were cold enough to be picked up, Noah took one and placed it in his slingshot. Holding it out in front of him, Noah pulled the inferno berry back against the sling. Glancing over his shoulder at Fletcher, he said, "You might want to get a little further back, my friend."

Grinning, Noah faced front and released the berry. Zipping from the slingshot, the berry raced through the forest until it collided with a tree trunk. On impact, the berry ripped open, releasing a blast of seething, blue energy, which sliced the tree trunk in two. The tree went crashing to the forest floor. All the trees surrounding it were scorched black, and some of them stood smouldering like candles that had just been blown out.

"Did you see that?" Noah gasped. *"Did you see that?"*

Stepping toward his friend, Fletcher looked into his eyes and said, "Noah, we must never do this again. We must never tell any of our friends what we have discovered."

Noah frowned. "Why not?"

"Because it's dangerous. Someone may get hurt or *worse*," Fletcher cautioned him.

"But..."

"No buts, Noah," Fletcher said. "Promise me you'll never tell anyone or..."

"Or what?" Noah challenged him.

"Or I will never speak with you again."

Seeing the seriousness in his friend's eyes,

and never wanting to lose his friendship, Noah lowered his slingshot. "You have my word."

Fletcher watched as Noah threw the rest of the berries into the river. They turned, and in silence, they made their way back to their camp.

A few weeks later, Noah had gone off through the Howling Forests alone and was never seen or heard of again. Some said they had heard a terrifying bang similar to that of an explosion come from some way away. The Moon Howlers had searched for Noah for weeks and no one could explain his strange disappearance – although most were happy that Noah hadn't come back. But Fletcher knew in his heart what had happened to him. Fletcher made a promise to himself that he would never touch another inferno berry as long as he lived.

So it was with some trepidation and a heavy heart that Fletcher reached out and began to pluck the berries from the inferno bush that Una had guided him to. He filled the pockets of his jeans with them, and when they were all full, he crammed the holdalls with as many as he could carry.

He took them to a nearby clearing and made himself a small fire. He felt about in the earth until he found himself a large slab of rock. Covering this with the inferno berries, Fletcher placed it into the fire. Cocking his head to one side, he waited and listened for the first sounds of hissing.

As he waited, he thought of his friend Noah again, and if he still had his eyes he knew they would be weeping. Hearing the faintest of *hisses*, Fletcher reached into the fire and withdrew the rock. While he waited for them to cool, he ripped the sleeves from his red checked shirt and knotted two of the ends. Scooping up large handfuls of the berries, he filled the sleeves with them. Once they were full, he tied the ends with pieces of twine, which he looped down and fastened to the knotted ends of the sleeves – making two slings. Fletcher then produced a small piece of paper and pencil from his pocket. He pictured the letters and words he wanted to write, and let his hand move over the paper. Without being able to see the words that he scrawled, Fletcher wrote two short notes and fastened them to the slings.

Once he had finished, he scooped everything together and made his way back toward the clearing where Abe, Marco, and Lacey still slept. Una led Fletcher into the small circular area. Sniffing each of them out in turn, Fletcher placed the items he had gathered on the ground. Resting the bow, sword, slingshot, and the inferno berries beside Marco and Abe, he hoped that they would both read the note attached before using them.

Knowing that he could do no more to aid them on their journey, Fletcher stooped over his sleeping son and whispered into his pointed ear. "I forgive you, son."

Without looking back, Fletcher commanded Una to lead him to the foot of the Snowstorm Mountains.

Chapter Fourteen

Knowing that his niece, Lacey had stepped through a mirror and into the world beyond it caused Victor a headache. The pain was a dull thud, but he knew if he didn't remedy the situation the headache would soon begin to pound and then beat against his skull. He knew Draconia had released the Guardians to dispose of Lacey, but it wasn't the thought of his niece dying a hideous and painful death that troubled Victor. It was the knowledge that Lacey would never be returning home.

Thea's illness, he could deal with. He could write the sick certificates himself and that would end any further inquiry, should anyone come snooping. But a *missing* young woman like Lacey? Not so easy. Unlike Thea, Lacey had gone to college. She still had friends in this town – although he had tried his hardest to put an end to any such acquaintances long ago. But what if a friend from her past should come calling? He could say she was ill? But that would only encourage them to come back to see if there was any improvement in her health. He could say that she had moved away. But what if he was asked for a forwarding address – a mobile number – details of a Twitter or Facebook page – weren't all young people obsessed with such things? He would have to know such contact details... he was her uncle, after all. If he couldn't provide these details, wouldn't people – the authorities – start to poke their noses into his affairs?

In some respects, Victor couldn't give a damn about who asked questions. They could ask all the questions they wanted – but not just yet. The time wasn't right. Once Thea and the Queen were both dead, he had planned to slit Lacey's throat while she lay unconscious in her bed, and then disappear through his mirror and never return. But until both Thea and the Queen were dead, he didn't want any interference from the authorities to scupper his plans.

Sitting at the kitchen table, Victor rubbed his temples with his bony fingers. The thuds inside his head had already turned into bangs and he felt as if he just might puke. Then Victor had an idea. He would report Lacey missing to the police. Yes! He would go to the police and say that his niece, still traumatized out of her tiny mind due to her parents' death, had got in with the wrong crowd – a crowd like the one that had once humiliated him – and had gone with them to London. He would report Lacey's disappearance to the police because he was out of his mind with concern for her. But he would need something – a letter left by Lacey in her own hand, declaring her unhappiness and desire to run away to London.

Grinning, Victor went to his study and found himself a piece of writing paper and a pen. Turning to his many bookshelves, he ran his fingers along the spines of the books until he found the one he was looking for. Pulling it from the shelf, Victor turned it over in his hands. The book was bound in corpse flesh and the pages were yellowed and dog-eared. Smiling, Victor looked down at the title: *The Primeval Book of Magic and Sorcery (Volume Six hundred and Sixty-Six).*

Victor didn't know who had written the book and conjured up the hundreds of spells and potion recipes within its pages, but he had a good idea. Araghney. He hadn't read or seen the other six hundred and sixty-five volumes either, and had often wondered what glorious and devious concoctions might be hidden within their pages.

Victor went to his desk and sat down. Placing the large book before him, he began to thumb through the pages. He scanned each page in turn as he sought out an appropriate spell. There were pages of curses and magical spells for all kinds of bewitchments. He saw it... just what he'd been looking for. With nervous excitement, he ran his finger across the page title and said aloud: "The Demented Hand of Deceit."

Scanning the page, he ran one crooked finger beneath the lines of words. He read them over and over again until he was confident that he could remember them. Once he was ready, he closed the book and sat back in his chair, closing his eyes. Picturing Lacey in his mind's eye, Victor felt repulsed at the sight of her. Swallowing back a mouthful of bile, he stretched out his right hand and began to say the words he had learnt from the book.

Lips flapping, he whispered the spell over and over again. The words and phrases circled the image of Lacey that he held in his mind. Lips moving faster and his voice becoming louder, Victor began to chant: "*Hand of girl, hand of decoy, give her fingers for me to destroy. Take her fist, take her gift, replace her knuckles with thy mist. Make my hand, change my hand, let it dissolve into grains of sand.*"

Chanting the words over and over again, spittle began to fly from his lips and splatter the back of the hand that he held out before him. As the spittle touched his paper-thin skin it began to bubble and blister. Over and over Victor repeated the words. His narrow chest began to rise and he tapped his feet in time on the wooden floor. Then, just as he had commanded in the spell, his fingers began to break up, shift and disintegrate into a fine shower of sand. Victor's hand fell apart and the sand blew about the room as if trapped in a tornado. The sand hovered in the air just above his sleeve where his bony hand had once been.

"Make it new, make it brew. Reform my hand, so it's delicate and true!" Spitting the last of the spell from his lips like poison, the grains of sand hovered for a moment then shot up his sleeve. Shaking in his seat, Victor gripped his arm with his left hand. He opened his eyes and stared down at the empty space. Then, as if by magic, five fingers began to ooze from the end of his shirtsleeve. These fingers were attached to a hand, which in turn, was attached to a wrist.

Looking down at his new hand, Victor sighed in wonder. He placed his left hand next to it, which was long and bony, with bulbous knuckles. The other was that of a young woman, smooth, slender, and unmarked. This was the hand of his niece. Feeling pleased with himself, Victor plucked up the pen and paper and began to write a letter as if written by Lacey's very own hand.

To my dear Uncle Victor,
Even though your kindness shows no

boundaries, and you have been a wonderful uncle to me and my sister, Thea, since the deaths of our parents, I have taken the decision that I need some time on my own.

However much I have tried, I cannot come to terms with the fact that my parents have gone, and as you know this has caused me great sadness. Thea is dealing with her grief in her own way and taken to her bed in a state of deep depression.

It hurts me to see you so worried about us and I am forever grateful to you for all the love and kindness you have shown Thea and me in your attempts to make us better. I therefore believe that if I were not around then you would be able to give her your full attention.

I want you to know that I have decided to run away to London where I hope I will be able to find the peace that I am looking for.

Please don't look for me as I know that this will take you away from all the love and support that you are giving Thea as she tries to deal with the loss of our parents. I just need to deal with that loss in my own way.

With all my love, dear uncle,
Lacey

Putting down the pen, Victor admired his cunning. He read the letter over and over until tears brimmed in the corners of his eyes then spilt down his emaciated cheeks. Placing the letter in an envelope, he couldn't hold back any longer and he sat and rocked with uncontrollable laughter.

Gripping his sides, Victor roared and he feared that he might just pee himself as the excitement that he felt bordered on ecstasy. Even as he stood and pulled on his overcoat, his lips trembled as he tried to control himself. He couldn't very well stroll into the local police station and report his beloved niece missing while he screamed with hysterical laughter. Placing the letter into his coat pocket, he rummaged through his desk drawers. He knew there were some pictures of Lacey in there somewhere. His idiotic brother would send him pictures each year so he could see how much they had grown. Victor had never put any of the pictures on show; he had thrown them into the drawer and forgotten all about them – until now. Now they would be useful to him. Now those pictures of his niece would be priceless. Spying one of Lacey under a pile of notes and old correspondence, he picked it up. Was it Lacey or Thea? They were identical. Did it matter? Placing the photograph in his pocket with the letter, he stepped out into the cold.

Victor was sure he had thought of everything. A letter in Lacey's own handwriting declaring her love for her uncle and her desire to run away, and a picture for the missing person's poster the police would want to make. But what about my hand? he thought glancing down at the long slender fingers protruding from his coat sleeve. With a sly smile, Victor shook his hand violently until it was nothing more than a blur – until it looked like his own once more.

Trying to stifle another fit of chilling laughter, Victor pulled his collar up against the snow that had begun to fall again and made his way into town.

Chapter Fifteen

Within minutes of waking, Lacey, Abe, and Marco had gathered together the supplies Fletcher had left them. They read the note he had attached to the slings, and looked at each other.

"Explosives? Handle with care?" Abe said aloud. "Use only if necessary!" Grinning to himself, Abe folded the piece of paper and stuffed it into his trouser pocket.

Without looking back, they left the clearing and made their way deep into the Howling Forests. Running between the trees and undergrowth, Lacey sensed an urgency from her two new friends. Abe led the way, his black and strange looking spectacles helping him navigate in the darkness. Through the dark lenses, Abe saw his path amongst the trees as if wearing a pair of night-vision goggles.

Lacey was still struggling to believe that just hours ago she had been unaware of the Mirror Realm and her new friends. No such place or people had existed to her. It seemed incredible to her that while she had been living in her world, lying drugged and close to death in her bedroom, Abe and Marco had been racing each night across the desert in search of the mirror that she was to step through. Another thing that puzzled her or rather troubled her, if she were being honest with herself was that Lacey didn't know if she was up to the task of saving Thea and the Queen. Lacey had never done anything heroic before, and the journey that now lay before her made her stomach churn and heart race. It wasn't that she feared for her own safety. What worried Lacey was that her friends seemed to have placed all their hopes on her saving their Queen and she didn't want to let them down. She didn't want to let herself down. For the time being, she tried to push those fears to the back of her mind. With the crossbows slamming against her thighs, Lacey ran behind Marco and Abe into the darkness that awaited them.

High up in the Splinter, Draconia stood at the end of the bed and looked down upon the Queen. She seemed almost lost in the huge, oversized bed. Her perfect white hair fanned out across two velvet pillows like wings. Her flawless face looked peaceful as she slept, unaware that her kingdom was being ripped apart. She had fallen asleep some years ago and her blue eyes hadn't opened since. Manoeuvring around the edge of the bed, Draconia's cloak whispered and shifted about him. It began to disintegrate, as did his flesh beneath it.

With his skeletal fingers, he took hold of the Queen's wrist and felt for her pulse. Just beneath her delicate skin he felt the faintest of beats. He grinned in the knowledge that every day now it grew weaker and slower. He let her arm drop onto the bed.

"Not long now, my Queen. I have the box and will soon have the key. It is only a matter of time before I have the shard of mirror that lies within it," he gasped. "And once I have it, your reign will end."

Shuffling away from the bed, Draconia went to a large set of bay windows. Pushing them open, he stepped out onto a balcony that jutted from the side of the Splinter. The wind grabbed at his dark robes and they fluttered about him like wings. Looking out across the desert, he felt a twinge of excitement gnaw away at his shrivelled heart. It wasn't just the knowledge that soon the whole of the Mirror Realm and the world beyond it would be his; it was the beautiful sight of his Guardians striding across the desert below him. Even though he stood miles above the desert, he could hear their feet thundering in unison as they began their search for the girl.

"*Lacey Swift*," Draconia hissed, blood

seeping from the corners of his grim smile.

Lacey came to a sudden stop in the forest. "What was that?"

"What was what?" Abe said, starting to slow and glancing back at her.

"I thought I heard somebody say my name."

"Well, it wasn't me," Marco said.

"Nor me," Abe added.

Lacey's flesh suddenly turned cold. She shivered, looking back into the darkness. "I'm sure somebody whispered my name. I heard it."

"You're just hearing things – it's probably just the wind you heard," Abe said. "Come on, I can see the trees thinning out over there."

Abe and Marco set off again and Lacey followed, but not before she had glanced back into the dark again.

They reached the edge of the Howling Forests to find themselves faced with a vast area covered with slabs of black granite stone. The slabs protruded from the ground like gravestones and disappeared into the distance for as far as the eye could see. They glistened in the rain that had started to fall and the moonlight glinted off their razor-sharp edges.

Without wasting any time, Abe started across the bleak and treacherous-looking landscape. A low wind groaned about them.

"What is this place?" Lacey asked, navigating her way through the bladed rocks.

"It's a graveyard," Marco said.

"I can see that," Lacey said back. "But I want to know..."

"Shhh!" Abe hissed. "You don't want to be disturbing them."

Lacey dropped her voice to a whisper. "Disturb who?"

"Them!" Abe suddenly said, pointing into the distance. He came to an abrupt halt.

Lacey stared in the direction that Abe was pointing. Several apparitions spiralled up from the ground like steam from an overflowing kettle.

"Stay still!" Marco hissed, gripping Lacey by the arm. "If you don't move they might not see you."

"Are they more of your people?" Lacey whispered, before yanking herself free of Marco's grip.

"Not my people this time," Marco said, without looking at her but straight ahead.

Lacey watched as the wisps of smoke floated up into the air and entwined with each other. Her heart began to thump so loudly in her chest she was sure the spirits, or whatever they were, would hear it.

The smoke began to separate like liquid and take on the form of several individual shapes. They twisted and contorted like tormented souls until they had taken on the silhouette of several young women who wore long, white, flowing dresses. Each of them had a white lace veil pulled down over their faces. They looked as if they were wearing wedding dresses.

"Who dare disturb our sleep?" one of them cried from behind her veil.

Lacey and her friends stayed perfectly still and silent.

"Who's there?" screeched another, her veil and long, flowing dress shimmering translucently all about her. "Who has come to taunt us, the vampire brides? Have we not suffered enough?"

Again, Lacey, Abe, and Marco remained silent, the rain lashing against them, running down their faces in icy rivulets.

Swooping through the rain, the long, flowing hems of the brides' dresses melted away, turning into wispy tails that floated behind them in tendrils. They hovered above the heads of Lacey and her two friends. Lacey's fingers twitched above the crossbows without her even knowing it. Abe glanced at Marco who in turn glanced at Lacey. The tension was unbearable.

Spiralling above them like a twister, the brides descended with such speed that Lacey wondered if they didn't possess the power to *blink*. The women suddenly appeared before Lacey, Marco, and Abe. The brides pressed their black and twisted fingernails to Lacey's and her companion's throats.

"Who are you? What is your name?" one of the brides screamed, pushing her pointed fingernails deeper into Lacey's flesh. Even though the bride's hands were see-through, Lacey could feel the bride's hooked claws pressing into her throat.

"Lacey Swift," she answered, gasping for breath, the bride's grip on her throat now suffocating.

Hearing her name, the brides reared back, and as they did, their veils blew up. Their faces were as white as the dresses they wore. The brides' eyes were black, lips crimson. They screwed up their faces as if consumed by pain.

"She's been sent by the sorcerer!" one of them cried.

"She's an agent for the evil one!" another screamed.

The bride who had taken hold of Lacey by the throat screeched. And as each of the brides released a cry of anguish, their lips rolled back in a grimace to reveal mouths that were full of spiked teeth.

Looking Lacey in the eyes, they pulled back their ghostlike claws as they moved to strike.

"Get back!" Abe snarled.

All seven brides whirled around in the air to find that Abe and Marco were now armed. Abe had snatched hold of the bow that he carried on his back. The tip of the arrow that he now pointed at the brides had one of the berries his father had gathered skewered to the end of it. Marco had drawn his sword and was holding it aloft before him. The blade looked sleek and razor-sharp in the driving rain and moonlight.

"We have brave ones here!" one of the brides hissed, a crooked smile stretching across her somewhat beautifully pale face. "Do you think you can hurt us with your weapons?"

The other brides began to giggle – the sound nothing more than a chilling whisper.

Aiming the bow above the brides' heads, Abe pulled back as far as his arm would go and released the arrow and the inferno berry. It whizzed up into the rain-soaked night, disappearing from view. All of them waited. Nothing happened.

Smiling at Abe, a bride said, "See, I told you..."

There was a hideous *cracking* sound as if

the very fabric of the night were being ripped open. Everyone flinched, their faces a mask of surprise. The night sky lit up in hues of electric blue. This was followed by an almighty explosion. All of them spun around just in time to see a shockwave of bright-blue, pink, and mauve energy *whoosh* through the air, slicing apart everything in its path.

"Fuck me sideways. I did not expect that!" Abe shouted. He dived for cover behind one of the huge slices of rock. Even the ghostlike-brides, who had been so confident in the knowledge that they couldn't be harmed, disappeared back beneath the ground.

Draconia's Guardians had raced through the night. Somewhere in the desert they had split, heading to the four corners of the Mirror Realm. Although setting off in different directions, all of them had one aim, one mission – to kill the young woman, Lacey Swift. They couldn't be bargained with. You couldn't reason with them, and pleading just dragged out the inevitable. The Guardians were heartless and soulless. They were ruthless killers, and each and every one of them wanted to be the one who took the head of Lacey Swift to their master.

As one faction marched east around the perimeter of the Howling Forests, the sky ahead of them exploded in a haze of blue electric light. Although they were some miles away, the earth beneath them vibrated. They came to a halt, their swordsticks thundering into the hard-packed ground of the desert. The lead Guardian screwed his red, bleeding eyes together and looked at the light that illuminated the sky like a flare. With the back of one claw, he wiped away the red tears that leaked from his eye sockets.

"We have her," the Guardian whispered, his fleshy lips rolling back like a snarling dog.

The lead Guardian held his swordstick above his elongated skull and roared, *"Charge!"*

On his command, the Guardians raced toward the light. Their boots sounding like thunderclaps rolling across the desert floor.

The last of the debris sent flying through the air by the exploding inferno berry rocketed over Lacey's head as she hid behind a giant slab of granite stone. The blue explosion of light and energy faded, and the aftershock rippled away.

"Your father wasn't kidding when he warned us about those berries," Marco whispered wide-eyed at Abe.

"He's full of surprises," Abe said, peering over the edge of the rock. "Those berries seemed to have done the trick and scared off those brides."

Lacey peeked over the jagged headstone she had taken shelter behind. She looked into the distance as the rain sliced through the darkness all around them. "I don't think we're out of danger yet," she warned, seeing the phantom brides coil up from beneath the ground again. Without thinking, Lacey reached down for her crossbows. Sliding them from their holsters, she gripped them in her fists.

From his hiding place, Marco noticed the fluid movement in which Lacey had drawn the crossbows. "Whoa, check out the Night Hunter all tooled-up and ready for action."

Glancing at the crossbows in her fists, then back at Marco, Lacey whispered in wonder, "How did they get there?"

But she didn't want to sound or look surprised – not in front of Marco. She wanted him to believe that drawing the crossbows had been a deliberate act on her part. She wanted both her companions to believe that she was ready for anything – any danger she might face on the journey she now found herself on.

The brides came soaring toward them again. Lacey was the first to spring from her hiding place. She thrust both arms out, elbows locking as she pointed the crossbows at the brides. Lacey reasoned that as the phantom brides had been so scared by the explosion, then perhaps they could be destroyed after all. She could still feel her throat stinging from where one of the brides had gripped hold of her. Although Lacey was new to this world, even she could figure out that however transparent the brides looked, if they could harm her, then they could be harmed, too.

"Stay where you are!" Lacey ordered the approaching brides.

As if surprised by the commanding tone of Lacey's voice, the brides swooped through the air, but didn't come any closer toward her. They hovered back and forth in the air some feet from her. Hearing the boldness in their friend's voice, Abe and Marco both looked at one another and shrugged. The brides eyed Lacey with a newfound caution and suspicion. They continued to circle her from a short distance away, wary now and not wanting to come too close.

"Sorcerer!" one of the brides spat.

"I'm not a sorcerer," Lacey said, crossbows still aimed at the brides.

"You lie," one of them sneered, upper lip rolling back to reveal her spiked teeth. "We know the name *Swift*. One of you came before."

"Victor was his name," added another. "He came with the sorcerer, Draconia. Because we refused to be Draconia's brides, he and Swift drove stakes into our hearts while we slept hidden away from the sunlight." As the bride spoke, a red shape began to blossom on her wedding dress just above her left breast. The same stain began to appear on all of them. As Lacey watched, she realised that the red patches was the blood seeping from their wounded hearts – from the holes made in them by the stakes Draconia and her uncle and driven into them while the brides had slept.

As Lacey began to gradually learn the true depravity of her uncle, one of the bleeding brides screamed, "They *cursed* all of us! We are now nothing more than spirits – *ghouls*. We will never become true brides. We will never know love or be loved."

Lacey swallowed hard. She could understand the young women's pain and eternal torment. Her uncle had tormented her, too. "It wasn't me who did that to you," she said, crossbows still pointed front, as the brides continued to circle her and her friends. "That was my uncle and I am nothing like him."

"I knew it!" the bride wailed, her veil flapping like tissue on the wind. "The girl and her friends are sorcerers who have come with magic to finish us."

"Listen to my friend," Abe said, stepping forward. "Lacey can save us all. She will one day be able to lift your curse."

The brides swooped around and around in the air. Lacey kept her crossbows trained on them. She daren't take her eyes off them for one moment.

"You lie!" a bride screeched. "How can this girl save us?"

"Lacey's sister – twin sister – is our Queen's replica. Thea Swift is the Queen's *reflection,*" Abe said. "We are looking for the box – the box that contains one of the Clicks."

Hearing this, one of the brides raced toward Abe. She stuck her claws to his throat. "And that's how I know you lie, Moon Howler," she heaved, her face just inches from his. "No one knows what is in the box. No one has seen inside it. How could you search for something that no one has ever seen?"

Spinning round, Lacey placed the tip of one of the crossbows against the bride's head. "Let my friend go," she commanded.

The bride didn't move. Lacey cocked the crossbow by rolling the hammer back with her thumb. "Let him go now," she whispered.

Feeling a dull pain in her side, Lacey looked down to see that one of the brides had crept up on her. The bride was now digging at Lacey's side with her long, jagged claws. *Blinking,* Marco appeared behind this bride, his sword at her throat.

"We have a standoff," the bride smiled.

Hearing this, the remaining brides swept forward and circled them.

"You can't win," the bride chuckled. "Now put down your weapons."

"Release my friend first," Lacey hissed in the bride's ear.

The bride tightened her grip on Abe's throat.

"I know what's inside the box," Abe suddenly said, staring at the bride from behind his dark glasses.

"Impossible," she sneered. "You lie to save your scrawny neck."

Tearing the black and peculiar-looking spectacles from his face, Abe said, "I've seen inside the box."

Chapter Sixteen

No longer wearing his glasses, Abe kept his eyes shut. He tilted his head back and then released a gut-wrenching howl. He sounded as if he were in agony. He opened his eyes. Tendrils of light oozed like serpents up into the night.

Seeing the rays of light streaming from his eyes, they all forgot the standoff. They lowered their weapons and claws, each of them taking several steps backwards. Their mouths hung open in shook and awe.

"I've seen inside the box!" Abe wailed, the wispy tendrils of light licking about his face. "I know what is hidden in there."

The brides looked at one another in total shock and confusion. *Blinking*, Marco appeared by Lacey's side. Looking at Abe, Lacey now understood why her friend had to wear those glasses. She remembered looking into those dark lenses and wondering what Abe's eyes had looked like. What colour were they? Where they green, blue, brown, or a fiery hazel? But this was something more – more than she could have ever imagined. It looked as if Abe's brain was on fire inside his skull and the flames had now been set free.

As if reading her thoughts, Marco said, "That's why Abe wears the glasses. It keeps the light from seeping from his eyes. It's the only way he is able to see. Otherwise he would be blind like his..."

Before Marco had a chance to finish, Abe had pulled the spectacles back over his eyes, trapping the leaking flames within his skull. The last of the thin, wispy lengths of white light were snatched away on the wind and gone forever.

As the tendrils of light from Abe's eyes had reached up into the night sky like vines, far away in their beds, both the Queen and Thea Swift sat bolt upright. They sat rigid, sweat glistening on their brows. Their hearts raced beneath their narrow chests and their heads pounded.

When Abe replaced his spectacles and the light vanished, both the Queen and her *reflection*, Thea Swift, flopped back onto their beds and sleep curled its dark fingers around them once again.

From behind the dark glasses, Abe looked at the brides. "We can find the box," he told them, sounding as if he needed to catch his breath. "And when we do, we'll return and with it remove the curse that Draconia has laid upon you."

"You never said what you saw in the box," one of the brides said, still sounding a little distrustful.

Abe ignored her question. "Do we have a deal or not? Can we continue on our way across your graveyard?"

The bride eyeballed him. "How do we know you'll keep your promise... how do we know that you will someday return and lift the curse..."

"Shhh!" Abe suddenly said, cocking his head and sniffing at the air.

"What is it? What can you smell?" Marco asked him.

"Trouble," Abe whispered.

There was a distant sound of rumbling. It sounded as if an entire army was heading straight toward them. The ground began to quake and the large granite slabs of rock shook. Sweeping into the air, the brides looked out across the graveyard. Their eyes grew darker as they peered through the rain and into the distance.

"Guardians!" one of them cried.

"But what can they want?" another wailed. "We're already cursed. Our sanctuary has already been destroyed."

"It's not us they want this time," a bride said, she turned in mid-air to face Lacey. "It's the girl they've come to destroy."

The remaining brides twisted in the air and raced back toward the ground.

"What's happening?" Lacey demanded, her crossbows gripped in her fists.

"You must go!" a bride said.

Seeing the fear in her ghostlike eyes, Abe and Marco armed themselves once more. The ground tilted and trembled beneath them. Then they saw what had panicked the brides so much. Over the brow of the graveyard, what looked like an army approached beneath the moonlight.

"Guardians!" Abe barked, taking aim with his bow and arrow that he had prepped with another berry.

"Who are they?" Lacey bellowed over the sound of the thunderous roar of the approaching Guardians.

"Draconia's protectors – his army. That's what they are!" Marco roared back, *blinking* forward to stand side-by-side with his friends.

The Guardians raced toward them, their eyes gleaming crimson in the dark. They approached in a solid formation and didn't once stop to navigate the razor-like rocks. Instead they smashed and trampled over them as if they were made of papier-mâché.

"Lacey Swift!" they screeched as one, their many voices floating on the air like a tidal wave.

"Go now!" the brides urged. "We will fight this battle for you!"

"But there are too many of them. There are only seven of you," Lacey shouted over the thunder of the approaching Guardians. Not knowing if she was saying the right thing or not, she added, "We will stay and fight with you."

Swooping in so close her transparent veil fluttered just inches from Lacey's face, the bride said, "It would appear, if what your friends say is true, the fate of the Mirror Realm lies in your hands, Lacey Swift. You're not destined to die today. Not if we, the vampire brides, have got anything to do with it. Besides, I have my own score to settle with these demons. *Now go!*"

"But you won't stand a chance! There are too many of them!" Marco roared, swinging his sword above his head in preparation for battle.

The Guardians were now within striking distance. Their eyes burnt red and plumes of grey smoke squirted from their puckered mouths.

"Lacey Swift!" they screamed, running forward.

"Go!" the brides screeched as one at Lacey and her friends. *"Go now!"*

Turning on their heels, Lacey, Abe, and Marco ran as fast and hard as they could away from the approaching Guardians. Zigzagging between the rocks, they tried to put as much distance as possible between them. Tripping over a jagged stone, Marco's hooded coat snagged and he became entangled. Running back toward him, Lacey and Abe fought to free him. Glancing back to see how close the Guardians were, Lacey watched the seven brave brides hold firm against the fast approaching army.

"Rise my beautiful sisters!" one of the brides cried out, raising her claws above her head. On her command the ground began to open as hundreds more spectral apparitions seeped up into the night. Each one of them wore a floating white wedding dress stained red with blood above the left breast.

"There's hundreds of those brides," Lacey whispered under her breath in shock and wonder.

The wispy streams of vapour swirled in – each tendril becoming a bride. They stretched across the graveyard for as far as the eye could see. The Guardians charged them, their swordsticks raised like javelins.

"Let's eat!" a bride screamed. "Let's drink!"

Abe yanked on Marco's coat until he heard the sound of tearing fabric. Freed from the rock, Marco thanked his friend. He looked back to see Lacey staring across the graveyard at the floating Brides. "Don't just stand there gawping!" he shouted at her. "Move your arse!"

Lacey turned her back on the brides and the approaching Guardians. As she raced away, she could hear the sounds of screaming as flesh was ripped from bone, throats were torn open, and blood was drunk. Abe bounded ahead on all fours, just as he had done in the forest when the giant wolves had attacked. Marco *blinked* his way across the graveyard. Every time Lacey drew level with Marco, he was gone again, reappearing several meters away. With her heart thundering in her chest and ears, arms working like pistons, Lacey propelled herself forward. Way behind her in the distance, she could hear the shrill screams of death. Lacey hoped those terrible cries of agony were the sound of the Guardians being slaughtered and not those of the brides. But she couldn't force herself to look back.

Abe stopped ahead. "I can see the shore."

Marco *blinked* the last few hundred yards and reappeared beside Abe. He glanced back over his shoulder at Lacey. "Hurry up!"

With a stitch burning in her side, Lacey forced herself onwards. She reached her friends and slumped forward, fighting to suck mouthfuls of icy cold air into her lungs.

"Look! Can you see it?" Abe said, pointing into the distance.

Looking up, Lacey could see they had reached the graveyard boundary. The razor-sharp rocks had come to such a sudden end it looked as if someone had erected an invisible wall. The rocks gave way to a cove of sandy dunes which sloped down onto a dark and deserted beach. All along the shoreline, thick, black waves like tar crashed against the sand.

"Is that the Onyx Sea you spoke of?" Lacey gasped, struggling to catch her breath.

"It certainly is," Marco said. "Now all we have to do is find a way across it."

"We better find a way quick," Abe said, staring past his friends and back across the graveyard.

Whirling round, Lacey and Marco looked in horror at the line of Guardians now racing toward them.

"They must have destroyed the brides," Abe shouted over the sound of the black waves crashing against the shore.

Lacey glanced down at the sea, which rolled to and fro like a giant oil spillage. It was then that she saw the mirror shining like a star in the darkness further along the beach.

"Look! There's a mirror!" she shouted, sprinting down the sandy dunes toward the shore.

Blinking his way onto the beach, Marco

was there before Lacey's leather boots had even touched the sand. Abe came bounding after them, thick plumes of breath pouring from his mouth like clouds. The mirror stood shining, the gloomy waves seeping beneath it.

With the wind rushing about them, they raced forward, the mirror getting nearer and nearer. Then something bright and orange soared over their heads and smashed into the sea, setting the waves alight. Without stopping, Lacey stole a quick look back to see the Guardians swooping down the sand dunes after them. They seemed to move at a terrifying pace and with every bloody heartbeat they got nearer. All along the crest of the sand dunes stood a vast line of the Guardians, and each of them had a seething fireball dancing between their fingers. In unison they launched the balls of flames from their fists. They rocketed through the night sky like comets, a blazing trail of burning light screaming behind them. With fireballs exploding in the sand at their feet, Lacey, Abe, and Marco raced toward the mirror. Clouds of sand erupted all about them as if they were navigating a minefield.

"They're almost upon us!" Abe roared, leaping past Lacey.

She didn't need to look back to know how close the Guardians were. Lacey could hear the sounds of their heavy footfalls right behind her and feel the hot air from their breath against her back. Pushing herself as hard and as fast as she could, she wondered if her heart might just explode in her chest. The mirror was so close now, Lacey refused to be caught this close to escape. Abe reached the mirror moments before her. He dived into it.

Marco *blinked* beside her and roared, "What are you waiting for, Lacey? Step into the mirror!"

Lacey looked into Marco's black eyes and could see the reflection of a firebomb hurtling toward him. Grabbing hold of Marco's hand, she dragged him into the mirror.

Lacey was sitting down. The chair was comfortable, though there wasn't very much legroom in front of her. She felt sick and disorientated. There was a loud humming noise, and it took a moment for her to realise it was the sound of engines – powerful engines. A voice cut through the fogginess, shrouding Lacey's senses.

"Good evening, ladies and gentlemen, this is your captain speaking," the voice said, and it sounded to Lacey as if it were coming through an intercom of some kind. "Please fasten your seatbelts as we make our final approach into London Gatwick airport. Thank you for flying Atlantis Airways."

Chapter Seventeen

Una saw the dome of blue light below through the snow that swept all around them. Fletcher smelt it and both of them shuddered under the sound of the explosion.

They stood on a jagged ledge of rock at the foot of the Snowstorm Mountains. The mountains towered above them, dark and menacing, forming a horseshoe around the eastern cove of the Onyx Sea. The mountain summits were hidden by purple-black clouds, bloated with snow. Wind howled all around them like the cries of ravenous wolves. Fletcher's once copper-brown hair now shone white beneath a coating of snow. Una barked and sniffed at the air.

"So it has started," Fletcher said, his words being eaten up by the blizzard that whipped all around them.

Una howled in response.

"We can only hope that they make it to the prisoner before they are captured," Fletcher added.

Snarling, Una shook a spray of snow from her sleek coat.

"I know, Una, but they have to make this

part of their journey on their own. We will have plenty of battles of our own to fight. Now lead on, my friend. We have work to do."

Pulling against her lead, Una led her master deep into the caverns of the Snowstorm Mountains. Within moments, Fletcher's enormous footprints had been filled with fresh snow, hiding any trace that either he or Una had ever been there.

The police officer handed Victor Swift the tissue and said, "Mr. Swift, please don't upset yourself. I'm sure your niece will be just fine."

Victor wiped his tear-stained cheeks with the tissue and then blew his nose into it. "I'm sorry for making such a fool of myself," he snivelled. "I blame myself."

"You have nothing to blame yourself for," the police officer said, completing the missing person's report.

"I just wished I'd noticed the signs. I knew poor Lacey had been unhappy because of her parents' tragic death, but I never in my wildest dreams thought she would run away – get in with the wrong crowd."

Shuffling his paperwork into a neat pile, the police officer looked at his watch. His shift ended in five minutes, and Manchester United was in a cup-tie with Chelsea tonight on the T.V.

and he didn't want to miss it – not one second.

Standing up on the other side of the table in the small interview room, the police officer opened the door.

"As soon as you've gone, I'll pass the picture and paperwork over to our force intelligence officer who will send out an all force report."

Sensing the police officer's wish to be rid of him, Victor wiped his eyes one last time for effect, and then placed the tissue in his pocket. Standing, he went to the door where the police officer was checking his watch again. Victor didn't care that the police officer wanted to get rid of him. He didn't want to stay in the police station any longer than he had to. He had never liked the police; they made him nervous.

"What's your name, officer?" Victor asked.

"Constable Moody," he replied, ushering Victor toward the door and out into the front office.

"You've been most helpful, Constable Moody. I'd like to write a letter of thanks."

Constable Moody checked his watch again. Two minutes until his shift ended. "There's really no need."

"I like writing letters," Victor added as the police officer opened the station door.

"Like I said, I'm just doing my job. I'll file

the report, and if we hear any news on your niece we'll be in touch."

"Likewise," Victor said, masking a smile in the knowledge that Lacey would never be returning home.

Constable Moody shut the door behind Victor. He glanced at his watch again. One minute to go. Running up the stairs to the locker room, he pulled his clip-on tie from his throat. Placing the missing person's report on top of his locker, Constable Moody got changed out of his uniform.

Victor thrust his hands deep into his coat pockets. *How fortunate I've been dealt with by such an incompetent and lazy police officer*, he thought to himself. He wouldn't even file that report, but that wouldn't be Victor's fault. He had done the dutiful thing and reported his beloved niece missing. Content, he smiled to himself and made the cold walk back to his cottage.

Slamming his locker closed, Constable Moody left the changing room. He got to the top of the stairs and then slapped his forehead with the flat of his hand. Running back to the changing room, he snatched the missing person's report from the top of his locker. Despite making himself late for kick-off, he dashed up two flights of stairs to the force intelligence office and handed in his report.

Chapter Eighteen

Without thinking, Lacey fastened her seatbelt as the pilot had instructed. Then it dawned on her where she was. The hum of engines, the uncomfortable feeling of turbulence, reminded her of the holidays she had been taken on as a child by her parents. "I'm on a plane!" she gasped.

Looking to her right, and if it hadn't have been for the seatbelt, Lacey would have jumped from her seat. Sitting beside her was the biggest wolf she had ever seen. It had a long, white snout, with black rings of fur around its eyes and ears. Its nose was black and wet-looking, and long, grey whiskers gathered around it. The animal's eyes were bright red with piercing black pupils.

"What are you staring at?" the wolf asked Lacey.

Fumbling for the clasp on her seatbelt, Lacey tried to distance herself from the wolf. "Did you just say something?" Lacey frowned in bewilderment.

"What's got into you, Lacey?" the wolf asked.

Hearing its voice again, Lacey realised she recognised it. "Abe… Abe is that you?"

"Of course it's me. Who else could it be?" the wolf said, its voice snarl-like.

Looking at Abe in disbelief, Lacey said, "Have you seen yourself?"

"What do you mean, have I seen myself?" Abe said, raising one giant white paw in front of his face. In shock, he added, "What's happened to me?"

"I think coming through that mirror has changed you. I think this is how you're meant to look in my world," Lacey said, narrowing her eyes and inspecting the wolf.

Placing the paw across his eyes, Abe said, "Where are my spectacles? How come I can see without them?"

"Perhaps you don't need them here – on this side of the mirrors," Lacey suggested.

"What about Marco? Where is he?" Abe asked.

Peering past Abe's huge frame, Lacey could see Marco bent double in the seat closest to the window. At first glance, he appeared unchanged, but then Lacey noticed Marco's back. It seemed hunched up; as if he was hiding something beneath the black coat he was now wearing.

"Marco, are you okay?" Lacey asked him.

Turning his head to look at Lacey, Marco's face seemed as beautiful as ever.

If not more beautiful, Lacey thought.

His dark eyes shone and his pale skin was as white as the moon. His skin almost had a translucent appearance, like it had been sculptured from the finest marble. Marco's hair framed his face in thick, black curls which shone so bright that Lacey had to close her eyes for a moment.

"I feel fine," Marco said.

It was then that Lacey and Abe both noticed Marco's teeth. Where he once had a perfect set, now protruded a pair of gleaming white fangs.

"What's happened to your teeth?" Lacey asked.

"What do you mean?" he said, popping his thumb into his mouth and prodding about.

"What the fuck!?" he cursed, withdrawing his thumb, which was now bleeding. Seeing the blood, he mopped it up with his tongue, licking his lips as if savouring some gastronomic delicacy.

"You've got fangs!" Abe barked. "You're a Blood Runner and not like other vampires. I've never seen you with fangs before."

But it wasn't the sight of Marco's fangs that disturbed Lacey as much as the sight of his now rounded shoulders. "What's wrong with your back?"

"I don't know," Marco said, in his usual offhanded manner. He twisted in his seat. "What are you talking about?"

"Does it hurt?" she asked him.

"Does what hurt?" he said, reaching round with one hand and touching his back. Then feeling a series of uneven bumps, he added with a look of surprise, "It feels as if I've got something stuffed up my coat. Hang on, where did this coat come from? This is not my coat! Where's my cloak?"

Lacey checked herself out to discover she was now wearing the trainers, jeans, and hooded sweater she had been wearing the day she came across the mirror in the woods.

"My old clothes are back," she said, glancing sideways at Abe, then back again at herself. "Where's the gauntlet... where have the crossbows gone?"

"Never mind the crossbows, what's that hideous humming sound? It's hurting my ears," Abe said, before flicking his now long, fleshy tongue over his snout.

"Oh, that's the engines," Lacey told him.

"Engines? What engines?"

"The things that are keeping us up in the air," she said.

"In the air?"

For the first time since meeting the strange werewolf, she thought that perhaps she could detect fear in his voice. "We're on a plane," Lacey said, as if he should have known this.

"A plane?" Marco asked, his fangs gleaming in the artificial overhead lighting above their seats.

"Yes, an airplane," Lacey said dumbfounded, suddenly realising her friends had no idea where they were. "We're flying through the sky."

"What?" Abe asked, his bright red eyes growing wide.

"We'll... yeah," Lacey said, bewildered that Abe seemingly had no idea what was going on.

"I don't like the thought of that," Abe snarled. He started to shift uncomfortably in his seat. "How high are we?"

"It's hard to say," Lacey said, glancing around the cabin. "This looks like a jumbo-jet so we could be flying as high as forty thousand feet."

"Forty thousand feet!" Marco exclaimed, dark eyes now as bright and wide as Abe's.

"I don't like it!" Abe groaned. "I want to get off!"

"You can't get off until we land," Lacey

told him with a bemused smirk on her face. Perhaps he and Marco now had some kind of appreciation as to how she had felt when first entering the Mirror Realm. "Everything you've seen in your world – the Wolf-gathers, the ghosts, those vampire brides... and you're frightened of a bit of flying?" Lacey teased. "You're a werewolf for crying-out-loud!"

Looking at her with his fierce, red eyes, Abe growled, "It's a shame you weren't this cocky when we were attacked by those Wolf-gatherers..."

"Well perhaps you can understand now what it was like for me to step into some fucked-up world where I knew nobody, where I was being chased by giant wolves that when dead became men, and then found myself in some godforsaken forest, where ghost-things were dropping out of the sky and popping up from beneath my feet..."

"Not ghosts – *Blood Runners!*" Marco hissed as he corrected her.

"Whatever," Lacey shot back. "Now you know what it was like for me, so quit complaining. You're going to draw attention to us. Besides, we'll be landing soon."

"I think it's too late for that," Marco whispered.

"Too late for what?" Lacey asked with a

growing sense of dread swelling in the pit of her stomach.

Marco nodded in the direction of the aisle. Lacey looked up to see a member of the cabin crew rushing toward them dressed in a shocking mustard-coloured uniform.

"How did you get that animal onboard?" the flight attendant demanded.

Lacey shot a look at Abe, then back at the member of cabin crew. She racked her brain for something to say – anything to explain away the fact that she was sitting next to a wolf. Very weakly Lacey said, "This is my pet." A nervous grin tugged at the corners of her mouth.

The member of cabin crew either didn't hear what Lacey had just said or simply chose to ignore it. She eyed all three of the odd-looking passengers. "In fact, how did any of you get on the flight? I've worked this plane since we left Orlando eight hours ago and I haven't noticed any of you before. Where did you come from?" Her pretty face became a mask of confusion.

"We've felt sick since take-off, and spent most of the time in the toilet," Lacey said, cringing, knowing that her explanation sounded pathetic.

Again, the young woman ignored Lacey. She was too busy staring at Marco. "What's up with your teeth?"

"My friend is waiting to have a brace fitted…" Lacey started.

"I'm not happy about this. Not one little bit," the stewardess said, shaking her head from side to side. "There's something wrong about you three. I'm going to have to contact the captain."

Before Lacey could say anything else – she had no idea what else she could have said to explain away their sudden appearance on an airplane traveling at forty thousand feet above the earth – the crew member had swirled around in a blaze of mustard and gone running back down the aisle.

"I think we're in trouble," Lacey said to her friends, her stomach somersaulting as the plane lost altitude and raced toward the runway.

Chapter Nineteen

As soon as the airplane's wheels screamed across the tarmac, Lacey released her seatbelt and jumped up.

"Somehow we've got to get off this plane or that's the end of our journey," she hissed at her friends.

"Why?" Abe asked.

Lacey felt exasperated. "Why? Because that lady has gone to tell the captain about us, and he will now be radioing the control tower, who will be calling the cops to meet us on our arrival."

Marco cocked an eyebrow at her. "Cops?"

Lacey sighed and said, "Venator Noctis – *Night Hunters* – or whatever it is you call them in your world."

"About time someone with some authority turned up. The Night Hunters won't harm us," Abe said, brimming with misguided confidence.

"I don't think they're going to be like the Night Hunters on the other side of the mirrors," Lacey warned him. She then looked at Abe and Marco and said, "God only knows what they'll make of you two."

"What's that supposed to mean?" Marco almost seemed to snarl at her, fangs glistening. He unfastened his seatbelt.

"All I'm trying to say is that I don't think the cops this side of the mirrors have ever been called to deal with a werewolf and a vampire on a flight before. Drunken football fans, yes. But not a werewolf and a vampire," Lacey said, crouching low so that she was almost on all fours and following the emergency lighting up the aisle.

Leaping from his seat, Abe sauntered up the aisle behind Lacey, his tail flicking back and forth. Bending almost in half, his back hunched as if he were concealing something under his coat, Marco followed. Passing the ends of the aisle, they were spotted by some of the other passengers.

"What the fuck is that!" one man shouted in disbelief. "It's a wolf!"

"Where? Where?" a female said, unfastening her own seatbelt and peering over the chair in front of her.

"Look, he's right!" a young girl chewing gum said, jabbing one finger in Abe's direction. "There's a wolf on the flight."

Other passengers began to release their seatbelts and stand so they too could get a look at the rapidly unfolding commotion.

"Hey, what's that guy hiding under his coat?" a young man said, pointing at Marco who was crawling on his hands and knees up the aisle.

"He's got a bomb!" a female screamed so loud that Lacey thought her ears were going to bleed.

"A bomb?" one of the cabin crew yelled.

"There's a bomb!" another crew member cried, running to the nearest toilet cubicle and locking himself inside.

Seeing this, other passengers began to scream and climb over their seats, heading toward the back of the plane so as to be as far away from Marco as possible. Within a matter of moments, the plane erupted into chaos and panic.

The pilot barked a series of orders at the air traffic controllers via his radio. The plane continued to taxi up the runway as the air traffic controllers closed all of the gates, and ordered the pilot to steer the plane away from the south terminal and to the end of the runway.

Reaching one of the exit doors, Lacey peered through the little oval window out into the darkness. In the distance, she could see the red and blue flashing lights of police and fire engines as they raced toward them.

Turning, she slumped against the door and slid to the floor. Looking at Abe and Marco, she said, "I don't know how we're going to get away."

For Lacey, it wasn't just the thought of having to explain away to the police what she was doing on the flight in the company of a giant wolf and a guy with teeth like a set of steak knives – she knew that they would call her uncle. She didn't mind the police doing so as she had every intention of going to them herself. She wanted to report her uncle for imprisoning her and her twin sister, Thea. But wouldn't she lose all credibility in the eyes of the police once she started to explain what she was doing on an inbound flight into the UK without a ticket, passport, and in the company of Abe and Marco? Sure, she could tell them about how she had stepped through a mirror into some strange parallel world, but the police and authorities would soon be bundling her up in a straightjacket and carting her off to the nearest asylum. How then would she ever get the police to believe her when she told them that Victor had been keeping her and Thea his prisoner for the last few years?

Seeing the alarm and fear in Lacey's eyes, Marco snapped at her in his usual bombastic manner. "Pull yourself together, Lacey. That door can be opened. We'll get off this plane."

Looking up, Lacey could see a list of instructions stuck to the inside of the emergency exit door, which started:

In case of emergency...

"Are you thinking what I fear you're thinking?" Lacey said, glancing at Marco. "Have you lost your mind? We can't open the door – the plane is still moving..."

"You have a better idea?" Marco said, brushing her to one side and taking control of the situation. It was this side of his manner that infuriated Lacey so much. She could feel her temper begin to boil again.

"You're staring at me again," Marco said.

And despite his arrogance and the fact that he now had fangs, Lacey couldn't help but still find him mesmerizing to look at – if not more so than before. Perhaps it was this that infuriated her so much and not his belligerence. "Why would I want to stare at you?" Lacey sniffed, looking away.

"Perhaps you would like to help me get this door open as it appears to be our only means of escape," he said.

With the help of Marco, Lacey followed the instructions, and with a *whoosh* of air, they forced the door open. The plane was still moving and, almost losing her balance, Lacey teetered on the lip of the doorway as the runway sped past below. Grabbing hold of her sweatshirt, Marco yanked Lacey back into the cabin.

"So what now?" Lacey roared somewhat smugly over the sound of the engines. "The plane is still moving too fast and we're way too high to jump. I knew this was a dumb idea, but you wouldn't listen…"

Beneath the sound of the screaming engines and the roar of the wind, which howled past outside, Lacey could just about hear the sound of tearing. Looking at Marco, Lacey could see his coat had begun to rip apart. As the fabric began to fall away in strips, Abe and Lacey stared in wonder as a pair of black wings unfolded from beneath Marco's coat.

"What the fuck?" Lacey breathed. "I didn't see that one coming."

Each wing seemed to have a long bony shoulder and arm that was about six feet in length. Beneath this arm hung the wing, which was a see-through and stretchy-looking membrane. Shaking from head to foot, Marco unravelled his wings. He looked from side to side and up at them.

"Wings?" he said, somewhat in awe of himself. "I have wings!"

Marco turned to face the passengers, who had now pressed themselves together at the back of the plane. The look of shock that had adorned his face on seeing his newfound wings was soon replaced with that sneer of arrogance again.

"See, I don't have a bomb. I have wings," he almost seemed to scold the petrified passengers. Then, taking control of the situation once more, Marco scooped Lacey and Abe up into his arms, and swept out of the doorway and into the night.

The stewardess in her mustard uniform stared in disbelief as Marco's big, black wings fluttered out of the cabin doorway. That was the last thing the stewardess saw before her legs buckled beneath her and she fainted in the aisle.

Swooping over the runway, Marco beat his wings up and down. But he soon began to lose height and spiral out of control toward the ground.

"You're too heavy!" he shouted at Lacey and Abe, holding them tight against him.

Feeling bruised by his comment, Lacey shouted at him over the driving wind and the whine of the plane's engines. "What are you trying to say, exactly?"

"I'm trying to say that we've got to land," Marco said, glaring at her, and tightening his grip about her waist and Abe's fur-covered flanks.

"If you hold me any tighter, you'll break my ribs," Lacey said, as his strong arm about her became almost crushing.

"Maybe you would like me to let go of you completely?" Marco said, suddenly loosening his hold on her.

Fearing that she might drop, Lacey squealed and tightened her grip on him. He grinned knowingly at her. She knew that he was provoking her and she hated him for it. Lacey hated the fact that he had the knack of making her feel foolish and helpless.

"You're such an arrogant and self-conceited dickhead!" Lacey spat at him.

"I can't hear you." Marco grinned. "Did you say something about wanting to see my dick? Because you know, I would love to oblige, but I really don't think now is the time. Perhaps later…"

Their eyes met. They looked at each other – perhaps a little too deeply, they both thought. Perhaps he liked feeling her close, and maybe she enjoyed being held against him, although she protested.

"I wasn't talking about your cock, you imbecile," Lacey yelled at him. "And believe me, there won't ever be a *later* for us!"

Still smiling to himself, satisfied that he

had riled Lacey, Marco looked back over his shoulder. His large, black wings beat powerfully up and down, yet he could feel himself being pulled down toward the ground. "I'm going to have to land," he said, more to himself than Lacey and Abe.

Fanning his wings out like two giant sails, Marco plunged out of the night sky and headed for the runway. Hitting the ground running, he released Lacey and Abe from his arms. Tumbling onto the runway, Lacey and Abe rolled over and over. Abe yelped as the pads on his paws skidded over the tarmac. Staggering to her feet, Lacey looked back at the police vehicles that were fast approaching – their emergency lights sending shadows across the airfield in flashes of blue and red.

"Run!" Lacey roared, heading toward the lights of the terminal that twinkled in the distance like some futuristic city.

Bounding after her, Abe's claws clacked against the surface of the runway. Soaring a few feet above them, Marco pounded his wings up and down like a giant bird of prey.

The police vehicles veered off the runway, making chase after Lacey and her friends across the grass, their sirens wailing and lights throbbing.

"Did you see that?" one of the police

marksmen asked the driver of the armoured vehicle.

The driver shook his head as if shaking away cobwebs and said, "I saw something fly from that plane but I'm not sure what it was."

"It looked like some kind of giant bat," the police marksman shouted over the din of the squealing sirens.

"Look! There they go!" the driver yelled, driving his boot down on the accelerator and speeding after them.

"It looks like that young girl is being chased by a wolf and that bat-thing," the marksman roared, peering through the windscreen of the armoured vehicle. He released the safety on his gun.

Lacey and Abe raced toward a stationary plane as Marco soared over their heads. Lacey and the wolf dived under the plane's giant wings. She glanced back over her shoulder as a synthesized voice came from one of the pursing police cars.

"STOP!" the voice ordered. "ARMED POLICE! STOP OR WE WILL SHOOT!"

"They can't shoot," Abe shouted, his eyes growing bright, tail whipping from side to side. "They're Night Hunters. They should be on our side – we've done nothing wrong."

"I keep trying to tell you, they're not Night

Hunters! They're *cops*!" Lacey panted, scrambling out from beneath the plane and running toward a hangar where trailers stacked with luggage were being driven.

"But we're the *good guys!*" Abe said, bounding after her.

"Somehow I don't think they will see it like that," Lacey gasped, drawing in deep lungfuls of air as she ran as fast as she could toward the open doors of the hangar.

The synthesized voice came again. "THIS IS YOUR FINAL WARNING! STOP OR WE WILL OPEN FIRE!"

Marco soared through the sky toward the entrance of the hangar. He glanced down and could see Lacey and Abe racing beneath him.

The air exploded with the sound of gunfire as the pursuing police officers opened fire.

"You weren't kidding!" Abe shouted, over the roar of a stream of bullets whizzing above his head.

"About what?" Lacey gasped in fright.

"They're nothing like Night Hunters. They're a crap shot," Abe said, bounding into the hangar.

Streams of smoke billowed up from beneath the tyres of the police vehicles as they came to a screeching halt.

"Alpha-Echo control! Alpha-Echo control from Whisky-Four-Five," one of the cops roared into his headset.

"Go ahead," a voice from the control room crackled in his ear.

"Subjects have decamped into the luggage store. I repeat, the subjects have decamped into the luggage store."

"Alpha-Echo control to Whiskey-Four-Five, seal the area, seal the area. We will contact the on-call negotiator."

Looking at his colleague in disbelief, the police marksman said into his mouth piece, "Whiskey-Four-Five to control... that's a negative. I repeat, that's a negative. I don't think a negotiator is going to be able to help. Perhaps you should call the nearest zoo."

There was a pause from the operator in the control room. Then the voice crackled in his ear again. "Alpha-Echo control to Four-Five, repeat your last message."

Sighing, the marksman spoke into the mouthpiece. "The hostiles appear to be a wolf of some sort and a giant bat."

The operator in the control room didn't respond for some considerable time.

Chapter Twenty

A bearded man wearing overalls shouted at Lacey as she came charging into the hangar. "Hey! You're not allowed in here! This is a restricted..." then he saw Marco fly into the hangar and the giant wolf skitter across the concrete floor. The baggage handler clamped his mouth shut, nearly biting off the tip of his tongue as he did so.

Snarling, Abe's lips quivered around his powerful jaws as he bounded across the hangar. Marco dropped out of the air, his large, black wings fluttering like shadows behind him.

"This way!" Lacey shouted, spying a conveyer belt that led up into the dark. The belt was ferrying hundreds of suitcases, prams, and rucksacks out of the hangar and up into the terminal.

Diving on to it, Lacey lay flat on her front as she was whisked upwards. Marco shrugged his shoulders as he walked toward the conveyer belt, his wings folding away beneath what was left of his coat. Climbing on, he was joined by Abe. The wolf's sharp claws scraped against the metal surface like nails being dragged across ice.

They were carried upwards through a maze of conveyer belts that stretched high above them like crisscrossing motorways. Ahead, Lacey could see a curtain of black rubber slats that brushed aside as the luggage passed through them.

At first, the passengers gathered around the luggage carousel in the terminal gasped at the sight of Lacey appearing on the conveyer belt as they waited for their luggage. Then the sounds of curiosity were soon replaced by screams as Abe and Marco appeared from out of the darkness. Brandishing his huge teeth, Abe snarled. Marco shook his shoulders again, unfolding his wings. Passengers fled backwards as Abe bounded from the belt and Marco swept up into the air.

On the runway, the police officers' radios began to crackle and hiss as frantic and garbled messages began to be transmitted.

"They now seem to be in the baggage area," said one hysterical controller.

"What terminal?" said the voice of a police officer.

"We believe they are in the north terminal," came another radio operator.

"Can we confirm the north terminal?" the police officer said again, his voice bubbling with frustration.

"No, I think they're in the south terminal,"

another voice cut over the rest.

Realising that no one had the faintest idea of where the hostiles were or what was going on, the fleet of armoured police vehicles split. One squad headed for the south terminal and the other headed to the north, their sirens and lights blazing as they hurtled along the runway.

As Lacey and her friends fled through the terminal, people scattered, leaving their luggage and belongings behind them. All around them, people dived out of their way as they raced through the terminal. Screams of terror could be heard in all directions as Abe howled through fear and confusion rather than to scare the passengers. Abe had never seen a place like this. Everything was so brash and lit with neon lights. The floor and walls looked artificial as if made from some shiny material and his snout was bombarded with the smell of cheap meat and sweet-things.

Fluttering overhead, Marco beat his wings, throwing-up abandoned newspapers and hamburger wrappers. Seeing the sign for Customs ahead of her, Lacey realised that she was heading in the direction of the exit. Lacey doubted very much if she would be asked if she had anything to declare, but then again, she wondered what the punishment would be for trying to smuggle a werewolf and a vampire into the UK.

The Customs officers, in their crisp, white shirts and starched trousers, heard the screaming before they even saw the young woman, wolf, and giant bat-thing. Their radios had been humming with news of them for the last ten minutes, and some officers had wondered if it were not some kind of joke. But as Lacey raced through the Customs area followed by the biggest wolf and bat they had ever seen, they all dived for cover beneath the x-ray machines and search tables.

Lacey raced toward passport control. The area looked pretty void of life except for a few Border Control officers who sat in little glass booths.

Border Control Officer Tom Smith shouldn't have even been working that day. He had been on leave, but when his supervisor had called him at home and offered him 'double-bubble' overtime to cover a colleague who had gone sick, he had been unable to refuse. However, when he saw the giant wolf come bounding toward his little booth, Smith wished he had never taken the call from his supervisor.

He can stick the money, he thought to himself, pulling down the blind on his booth and curling up in the corner. Through his fingers, he watched the shadow of the wolf go bounding past and a large black shape go streaking overhead. To his shame, Border Control Officer Tom Smith felt a damp patch form in his trousers. In that moment, he vowed that he would never answer his phone while on leave again. Lacey and her two odd-looking companions tore through the terminal.

Where to now? Lacey thought to herself, looking around. She knew that Marco and Abe would have to get far away from the airport – and quick. Spotting a sign for the *Gatwick Express Train*, Lacey shouted at Abe and Marco to follow her.

Lacey raced down the escalators, taking two steps at a time. Marco hovered behind her, his feet not touching the moving steps. He had never seen such a thing. Lacey reached the bottom to find a train at the platform edge. Looking up at the departure board, she could see that it was destined for London Victoria Station. Marco stepped down onto the platform. Lacey watched as he shrugged his shoulders again, wings folding away like the soft-top roof on a sports car. Marco couldn't help but notice the look of wonder he could see in Lacey's eyes, and he liked it.

Lacey looked away and boarded the train. She didn't want Marco to think for one moment that he might have impressed her. She knew his ego didn't need any more pampering.

Marco, still on the platform, called after her. "Where's Abe?"

Lacey poked her head through the open doorway and looked along the platform but couldn't see Abe anywhere. She then heard a pitiful yelping sound coming from the top of the escalators. Lacey stepped off the train, following the sound. Reaching the foot of the escalators, Lacey looked up to see Abe cowering at the top of them.

"What's wrong?" she asked the oversized wolf.

"The stairs are moving," Abe shouted, red eyes narrow slits.

Lacey shook her head as if unable to believe what she was hearing. "So, they're moving. What's the problem?" she asked.

"I've never seen moving stairs before."

"I don't believe this," Lacey sighed under her breath, making her way back to the top. How could Abe – a werewolf from a world that seemed to be home to so many freakish and terrifying creatures – be so cautious of a few moving steps? It didn't seem credible.

Taking hold of the fur around Abe's neck, Lacey tried to pull him down the escalators. From below she could hear the *bleeping* sound as the train doors prepared to automatically close.

"Come on, Abe. Shift your arse. Stop being such a coward," Lacey shouted at him. "We don't have time for your fun and games."

Squeezing past Abe's hulking frame wedged at the top of the escalators, Lacey placed both of her hands against the wolf's huge back legs and began to force him down the escalators. Snarling, Abe skittered on his long claws, lost his grip, and tumbled to the bottom. Lacey raced behind the toppling ball of fur. At the bottom she jumped over Abe, darting between the closing doors of the train. She thrust her arms out between the doors, preventing them from closing.

"Hurry!" Lacey yelled at Abe, who lay looking dazed and confused in a heap at the foot of the escalators.

The doors *beeped* as they struggled to close on Lacey.

"Get up, Abe!" Marco ordered, who had now joined Lacey in the doorway, helping her to keep them open. The gears in the inner workings of the door made a grinding and churning sound as they fought to close on Lacey and Marco.

Shaking his large head, Abe rolled onto all fours and leapt toward the closing doors. Lacey stooped as Abe bounded over her and into the carriage. Releasing their grip on the doors, Lacey and Marco leapt backwards as they hissed shut.

Then the screaming started all over again as the passengers caught sight of Abe for the first time.

Lacey raced through the carriage as people curled up in their seats, desperate to keep out of the way of the massive wolf-thing. The train listed from side to side as it sped over points and raced toward London. The three of them ran through the carriages until they reached the First Class compartment at the front of the train. This carriage was quieter and occupied by just one passenger who lay slumped asleep in one corner, a set of oversized earphones covering his ears. The hiss of distant music bled faintly from them.

"It's not going to take those police officers long to figure out what happened to us," Lacey told Abe and Marco.

"How will they know the way we are heading?" Abe asked.

Lacey looked at the wolf then at Marco. "Can't either of you change – you know, look more normal – human? If only you could look like everyone else we wouldn't stand out so much – draw so much attention to ourselves."

"I don't think we can change back…" Abe started.

"It would seem that by stepping through the mirror we have changed – become something that we are not in the Mirror Realm," Marco said.

"So you're both stuck like that?" Lacey said, the situation becoming more hopeless with each passing moment.

"Until we go back through the mirrors," Abe said, his voice deep and booming.

"We told you that the mirrors have a way of changing supernatural beings that pass through them," Marco said.

"Is that why my clothes have changed?" Lacey asked him.

"Perhaps," he said, with a shrug.

"But I'm not like you – I'm not supernatural. I left these clothes back in the forest by the fire…"

"Look, I don't know the answers to every goddamn thing," Marco said. "But what I do know is that we have to get back…"

"But how?" Lacey asked, not so sure now that she wanted to head back to the Mirror Realm, however bleak her immediate future seemed to be on this side of the mirrors.

"What I want to know is how you can be so sure those Night Hunters – cops – will figure out where we're heading?" Abe asked.

"CCTV. That's how." Lacey sighed, peering out of the train windows into the darkness.

"CCTV?" Marco asked, gripping the handrail as the train lurched this way and that.

"They are cameras that watch everything

you do," Lacey said, glancing up at the small, black lensed camera set above the vestibule door. Lacey sensed that neither Abe nor Marco had the slightest idea of what she was going on about. She had no idea how to explain what CCTV cameras were nor their purpose. She scratched her head and moved away from the door. "They are like mechanical eyes that watch what's going on. It's for security. It makes people feel safer. But then again, it just makes you feel like you're being spied on."

"Mechanical eyes?" Marco asked. He looked uncomfortable at the idea of being watched. Lacey stole some secret delight from seeing his reaction. Perhaps now he would begin to understand how she had first felt in the Mirror Realm.

"And I thought it was only my world that was full of magic," Abe said.

"It's not magic," Lacey said, perhaps more condescendingly than she had intended. But why shouldn't she marvel, for a moment at least, in their discomfort? They had shown little patience with her when she had being struggling to make sense of the new world she had found herself in.

"Can I take some of these magical eyes back into the Mirror Realm for my father?" Abe asked.

Lacey couldn't be sure whether Abe was

being sarcastic or whether he genuinely was thinking of his father's blindness and wanting to take something back to help him. She frowned back at Abe. "No you can't. The cameras are not magical and they don't work like that."

Lacey peered out of the window again, looking for any landmark that might suggest how far from London the train was. But the night was black outside and all she could see was her own reflection peering back at her from the window. Her reflection looked distorted, like she was peering into a broken mirror.

"What do you keep looking for?" Marco asked, stepping close behind her. He leant over her shoulder and looked out into the night. He was so close that Lacey could feel his cool breath against the side of her neck.

The sensation made her skin tingle. She eased herself away from the door and Marco. "I want to see if we are slowing down... to see if they've worked out what has happened to us. They might stop the train and then we'll be trapped."

"What sort of beast pulls this *train?*" Abe asked.

Lacey rolled her eyes. Was Abe being deliberately dumb to annoy her? Or were his questions any dumber than the multitude of questions she had asked of him when first stepping into the Mirror Realm? Knowing that she should perhaps give him a little more leeway, she said, "There isn't a creature pulling this train. It doesn't work like that. We haven't used animals to pull vehicles for years."

"So how does this huge beast move at such an incredible speed?" Abe pushed.

Lacey eyed him with suspicion. Did Abe really not know how a train moved or what it was? "It's not a beast. It's a machine like the plane we were on. It has an *engine.*"

Lacey didn't want to appear impatient – any more impatient than Abe and Marco had been with her in the Mirror Realm – as she suspected she understood what Abe and Marco were going through. They were just as confused and bewildered by this strange new world as she had been when stepping through the mirror. But now wasn't the time for questions. Just like the time hadn't been right for the questions she had pestered Abe with as they had raced toward the Howling Forests on the stagecoach. Looking at the world through Abe's and Marco's eyes, Lacey guessed that this side of the mirror was just as magical as the side they had come from. It was a different kind of magic that was all.

"Can I take one of these *engines* home?" Abe asked. "They sound incredible. What do you feed them on?"

"Now you're just taking the piss," Lacey sighed.

"If this train is anything like the one I've heard of in the Mirror Realm, the engines breathe steam and belch clouds of thick, black smoke," Marco said.

"You're talking about steam trains," she said, cocking one eyebrow at him. "Do they exist in your world?"

"I've only heard rumours," Marco said, looking slightly more confident as if he wasn't as naïve to this world as Lacey suspected him to be. "I've heard people talk of a machine – like the one we now travel on. It's made of iron, big and black. Some call it the Scorpion Steam. I have never seen it, but..."

Before Marco had the chance to finish, Lacey had pressed one finger to her lips. "Shhh! We're slowing down."

The train made a hissing sound as the driver applied the brakes and the train slowed. Lacey pressed the palms of her hands against the windows. Turning her head, she tried to see what was happening ahead. She could see the lights and the many platforms of Victoria Railway Station. The train rolled to a juddering stop. Lacey went and stood by the doors. As soon as they had parted, she poked her head out and peered along the platform expecting to see it teeming with British Transport Police officers, but there were none.

Stepping onto the deserted platform, Lacey urged her two friends to join her. Leaving the sleeping passenger unaware that he had just taken a ride with a werewolf and a vampire, Marco and Abe stepped down from the train and onto the platform.

Wide-eyed, Lacey looked at them and whispered, "Something isn't right."

Chapter Twenty-One

"What do you mean?" Marco asked, doing that thing with his shoulders again and unfurling his wings.

Lacey wished he hadn't. If he kept his mouth shut, hiding his fangs, then apart from his unnatural good looks, he wouldn't draw too much unwanted attention. But with his wings out, Marco was going to attract all kinds of attention – the wrong kind. But she knew there was little point in telling Marco any of this. She knew that he was too bombastic to listen to anything – or advice – she might have to offer, despite being on her side of the mirrors now.

She took a deep breath. "This is a busy commuter station in the heart of our biggest city. It should be teeming with people, but look, no one else has got off the train."

"Maybe they know something we don't," Abe said.

"That's what worries me," Lacey frowned, leading them along the platform and onto the desolate concourse.

"We should keep to the sides," Marco whispered, in an attempt to take control of the situation.

Lacey suspected that Marco had no real way of knowing how to control anything here. He was no longer in his world. The world was different on this side of the mirrors. "Why should we keep to the sides of the concourse?" Lacey asked him.

"We're less easily seen that way," Marco said, as if she should have already figured such a simple thing out for herself.

Despite her resentment for him, Lacey knew that Marco was right. She therefore, along with Abe, who crept at her side, made their way around the edges of the concourse pressed against the shop windows. They had gone halfway round when somebody shouted at them through a loudhailer.

"THIS IS THE POLICE. STAY WHERE YOU ARE!" the voice commanded, echoing off the floor and walls of the station. "PUT YOUR HANDS IN THE AIR SO WE CAN SEE THEM!"

Abe looked down at his paws and then at Lacey. "These cops of yours are far too dumb to be Night Hunters. I don't have hands."

There was a moment's silence before the voice came again.

"MOVE INTO THE CENTRE OF THE STATION CONCOURSE. KEEP YOUR HANDS WHERE WE CAN SEE THEM. ANY PERCIEVED HOSTILITY WILL BE MET WITH LETHAL

FORCE!"

"Marco can't you *blink* your way out of this?" Lacey asked.

"I don't seem to have that ability here," he said. "I think it has been replaced with wings."

Before Lacey could say anything else, Marco had sprung forward, swooping up into the air. "I'll draw their fire. Now get out of here!" he shouted over his shoulder at Lacey and Abe.

The gunfire started the moment Marco had darted from his hiding place and soared up into the shadows of the station's high ceiling. Across the concourse, Lacey could see a gated exit which led out into the street.

Pointing at it, Lacey said to Abe, "Look over there. Head for that gateway." Together, they darted from the shadows of the shop doorway they had been hiding in and headed for the exit.

Gunfire sizzled all around them as a volley of bullets ricocheted off the tiled floor. Spiralling up into the roof of the station, Marco spied the police marksmen hiding on the upper gantries. He watched them take aim at his two friends as they raced toward the exit below. Marco swooped down, knocking the marksmen from their perches like gargoyles on top of a cathedral. The officers cried out as they were struck from behind and sent pin-wheeling through the air.

Some of the other police officers saw their colleagues flying toward the ground and began to spray a hail of bullets up into the darkness. Pressing himself flat against the metal beams of the roof, Marco smiled. He knew he was too quick for them. Peering from the safety of the shadows, he sought out a new target. Looking like a giant raven, Marco plunged down out of the darkness, driving the police officer from his hiding place. The last thing the police officer would recall before writing his report later that night, was a pair of drooling fangs racing toward him.

Lacey and Abe dodged the bullets that rained down on them. Bounding in huge leaps across the concourse, Abe snarled, bearing his ferocious teeth for all to see. One of the police marksmen peered around the corner of a sandwich kiosk and Abe raced toward him. The officer's eyes grew wide with fear, and he froze on the spot like a waxwork. Seeing his chance, Abe stood on his hind legs and towered over the police officer. Standing like this, Abe was at least eight foot tall and ripped with muscle. With one powerful arm, he swiped at the officer, sending him flying through the glass windows of the kiosk. The police officer landed face down in the middle of the sandwich counter, slices of ham, cheese, bread rolls, and a dash of mayonnaise spraying up into the air.

Throwing his arms out on either side and making fists with his claws, Abe rolled his head back and howled. The noise was so loud that the windows in the nearby ticket booths and shops began to shatter and rain down from the roof above. Shards of broken glass showered down like daggers. The remaining officers ran for cover.

Abe roared, "Leave us alone! We haven't done anything wrong!"

Dropping onto all fours, Abe snarled once more in warning as he headed back to Lacey, who stood frozen with fear in the centre of the concourse.

"Run, Lacey! Run!" Abe shouted at her.

Seizing his chance, Marco dived toward the ground, his wings rippling behind him. His friends ran toward the gated exit. Abe bounded into it and the metal bars rattled in their frame.

"It's locked!" Lacey shouted, looking wide-eyed back over her shoulder for any signs of police officers.

"Not for long," Abe snarled, wheeling round and taking a run at it.

Throwing his full weight and muscle against the gate, it broke free from its hinges and flew into the street. Without hesitating, Abe bounded out. The sound of car drivers blasting on their horns soon followed. Marco hurtled from the station and soared up into the night.

Lacey took one last glance over her shoulder before facing front again and heading toward the gate. Everything happened so fast, Lacey didn't even have a chance to react. The gloved hand shot from the darkness and wrapped itself around her neck. Spinning round and backwards, Lacey went sprawling onto the concourse floor, smashing her head against the concrete with a sickening thud. Staring up into the face that looked over her, Lacey's eyes lost their focus and everything went black.

"I've got one of them," the police officer shouted into his radio.

Police sirens wailed in the distance as more units raced toward the railway station. Stooping closer to his prize, the police officer said, "Well I'll be dammed. I was only reading about you this afternoon on the briefing system. You're that young woman who has been reported missing."

Chapter Twenty-Two

Victor's head throbbed and the constant squeaks of the windscreen wipers were doing little to ease the pain. He raced down the M5 toward London, the tyres of his car hissing over the wet tarmac. It was almost midnight when he had received the call from the police station an hour ago.

"Mr. Swift?" the voice had said on the other end of the phone.

"Yes!" Victor had snapped. He had given Thea her evening dose of medicine and he had settled into his favourite seat before the fire, and had begun imagining his mirror when the phone had started to ring.

"Hello, Mr. Swift. My name is Superintendent Declan Tanner from the Terrorism Investigations Unit at New Scotland Yard."

"Oh?" Victor said.

"You reported your niece, Lacey Swift, missing."

"Yes, that's right."

"We'll, I'm pleased to tell you that we have found her," Tanner said.

"Okay," Victor said, flummoxed by this news. "What did you say your name was again?"

"Superintendent Tanner from the Terrorism Investigations..." Tanner started to repeat again.

"Is it commonplace for such a high-ranking officer from the Terrorism Unit to get involved in a missing person's enquiry?" Victor asked, his eyes forming into two narrow slits.

"Well, no, not normally, but this doesn't seem to be a simple missing person's enquiry."

Hearing this, Victor's lips went dry and the hairs prickled at the base of his neck. "How so, Superintendent?"

"Your niece was discovered to be on an inbound flight into the UK from the United States of America."

A difficult silence followed as Victor's brain started to jiggle about in his skull. "I'm really not sure what to say, Superintendent. I'm lost for words. Was she – Lacey – with anyone else?" Victor asked.

"Look, Mr. Swift, it would be much easier to go over this at the station. Would it be possible for you to come down to the Yard tomorrow? I understand that you're in Cornwall. Perhaps you could make it by lunchtime?" The last part of Tanner's sentence was given more as an order than a suggestion.

Victor's skin crawled at the thought of going back into a police station, and this wasn't any ordinary police station; this was New Scotland Yard he was being summoned to.

"Yes. Yes, that will be fine," Victor replied, beads of sweat beginning to dribble off his brow.

Victor was just about to say goodbye and slam down the phone – he was desperate to end this conversation just in case he was asked any difficult questions – when Tanner said, "Apart from the bump on your niece's head, she's doing okay."

"Sorry?" Victor said, flustered. Why wouldn't this cop just fuck-off?

"It's just that you went to all the trouble of reporting your niece missing but you haven't once asked if she is okay," Tanner said.

Victor detected a certain cunning about this officer. He wasn't lazy and incompetent like Police Constable Moody had been. This one was sly, loved his job, and was clever. He probably enjoyed beating himself off while wearing his pristine uniform. This Tanner sounded like he enjoyed the power of being a cop.

"How silly of me," Victor said, with a grimace, like he had swallowed a throat full of poison. "This has come as a bit of a shock and I'm not thinking straight. I'm still distraught that Lacey would have gone missing in the first place."

"I understand," Tanner replied.

"Is she in custody?" Victor asked, his eyes thin dark slits.

"No. Lacey is in St Thomas's Hospital nursing a sore head, that's all. She should be discharged tomorrow."

Why couldn't she be dead? Victor thought to himself and then said down the telephone, "That's such a relief. I will leave for London first thing tomorrow morning." Grimacing once again as if in utter agony, he added, "I look forward to meeting you then, Superintendent."

He placed the receiver back into its cradle. Throwing on his coat and grabbing his car keys from above the fireplace, Victor slipped from the house and wasted no time in racing toward London.

Rubbing his temples with his gnarled fingers, Victor peered through the rain that hammered against the car windshield. He glanced at the clock that glowed green above the dashboard in the dark. It was 01:45.

Wanting to be in London before dawn, he pressed his foot against the accelerator and sped faster down the motorway. Victor had already decided that he had no intention of going to meet with this Superintendent from the *Yard*. No sir-ree. He was going to go straight to the hospital, collect his meddling niece, and take her back into the Mirror Realm.

Draconia would know what to do with Lacey, Victor thought to himself. He grinned. But what would Draconia say?

It wasn't Victor's fault that Lacey had managed to come back. Draconia was meant to be taking care of that. Draconia had sent his Guardians to kill her. Victor's headache began to ease a little as he began to proportion the blame. But what about that interfering cop? Wouldn't he come sniffing around? There'd be questions to answer. Like how had his niece ended up on an international flight? And that cop knew more than he was letting on. That's why he wanted a meeting in London. There was more going on and that cop just wanted to watch him squirm under a bright light in some filthy interrogation room. Well it wasn't going to happen. He would flee into the Mirror Realm earlier than planned.

But what about Thea? He would have to take her, too. *But could she go through the mirrors? Hadn't Draconia forbade it, as it could cause complications? Wouldn't the Queen grow stronger if Thea was taken into the Mirror Realm? Hadn't Draconia said that they should only be brought together when they were both ready to be murdered?*

Victor's head began to pound again.

"Draconia will know what to do," Victor whispered to himself, trying to sound as confident as possible. "He'll know what to do."

Victor pressed harder on the accelerator.

Chapter Twenty-Three

Lacey opened her eyes. She was lying on a bed in a room with white painted walls. The smell of disinfectant was so overpowering that it made her eyes and nose sting. Lacey tried to lift her head from off the pillows, but lowered it again as a bolt of pain skewered its way into her brain.

"Ouch!" she murmured, the pain making her feel sick.

"Take it easy, young lady," said a voice.

Looking down the length of the bed, Lacey could see a stranger sitting at the foot of it. The man had steel-white hair and a big handlebar-shaped moustache to match. His eyes were an icy blue and framed with jet-black eyebrows that were in complete contrast to his white hair and moustache. He looked like a photographic negative. Despite his hair colour, his face looked younger, as if in his early forties. It was tanned as if he had just travelled from a very hot climate. He wore an expensive-looking suit with a matching tie.

"Where am I?" Lacey croaked, her mouth feeling dry and throat sore.

The stranger stood up. He was tall about six foot and slender. He poured a glass of water and handed it to Lacey.

"You're in hospital," the man said, propping up Lacey's pillows so she could take a sip of the cool water.

"In hospital?" Lacey asked, confused, head muddled.

"Don't you remember what happened?" the man said, stroking his overgrown moustache with a set of thick fingers.

Ignoring his question, Lacey said, "Who are you?"

"I'm a police officer. My name's Declan Tanner. Dec to my friends."

"What do you want?" Lacey asked, taking another sip of the water.

Sitting on the edge of the bed and meeting her with his cold blue eyes, Tanner said, "First, I want to know how you got onto that plane. I've checked with U.S. Customs and you didn't board the flight in Orlando."

Lacey refused to meet his gaze. "And second?"

"I want to know what the wolf and the bat-thing have to do with all of this."

"Shouldn't I have a solicitor or something before I answer your questions?" Lacey asked, "Isn't that what happens on the T.V.?"

Tanner smiled. "Look, I'm not treating you as a criminal. As far as I can see you're the victim. I just want to know how you got onto that flight."

Placing the cup of water on the bedside cabinet, Lacey winced at the pain in the back of her head. Once she had made herself comfortable again, she said, "You wouldn't believe me if I told you the truth. I can hardly believe it myself."

"Try me," Tanner said, folding his thickset hands in his lap.

"I came through a mirror."

"A mirror?"

This is where I get warned for wasting police time, Lacey thought to herself. *Or dragged off to the nearest asylum.*

"Go on, you have my complete attention," Tanner told her.

Lacey eyed him and then continued. "I came from a world called the Mirror Realm. I'm not some kind of weird creature or anything like that. I'm human. My twin sister, Thea, and I have been living with my uncle since my parents died in an accident. They were out walking – they got too near to the cliff edge…" Lacey trailed off. She reached for the glass of water and took another gulp of it. She didn't want to dwell on her parents' deaths. She couldn't change what had happened. Nothing would bring them back. But she could change what was happening to her sister, Thea. The cop who was sitting at the end of her bed seemed reasonable enough. Hadn't she yearned for this moment – to escape her uncle and tell the police about him? "My uncle is weird," she suddenly blurted out. "He's been giving me and my sister odd-looking pills. He says he's a doctor but I'm not so sure." Lacey paused and seeing that Tanner hadn't taken his eyes from off her, she added, "Shouldn't you be writing this all down or something?"

"Go on with your story," Tanner said.

"Ok. Where was I? Ah, yes. Anyway, I managed to get out of my uncle's house and I found this mirror sticking out of the ground in the woods near to my uncle's cottage. I stepped into the mirror and into a world called the Mirror Realm. It's kind of like a reflection of this world but it's being destroyed by some evil freak called Draconia. Draconia is my uncle's *reflection*."

"*Reflection?*" Tanner asked, with a smile twitching beneath his droopy moustache.

"Some of us have *reflections* in the Mirror Realm. Anyway, I made friends with this... someone called Abe. He has a lot of hair. Then there was this guy called Marco – really loves himself – I guess you know the type – and he could move fast from one place to another. He called it *blinking*."

"Blinking?" Tanner mused, with a half-smile.

Lacey realised she had been gabbling again. Perhaps Abe and Marco had been right about her after all – she did talk a lot. She talked way too much, once she got started. Lacey looked at Tanner. She cringed. "You don't believe a word of this do you?"

Tanner looked at Lacey for what seemed like forever. When the silence became so unbearable that Lacey felt like screaming, Tanner stood up and said, "I think you need some rest. You received a very nasty bump to the head. Perhaps you're not thinking so straight right now. I would, however, like to speak with your uncle before we chat again."

"My uncle is involved in all of this. I know you think I'm insane, or that perhaps I hit my head harder than you first thought, but you've got to believe me, my Uncle Victor is trying to kill my sister and the Queen."

Tanner raised his big black eyebrows. "The Queen, you say?"

"Not *our* Queen – not Queen Elizabeth," Lacey said, feeling foolish – feeling like a liar. "My uncle is trying to kill the Queen of that world I told you about – the Mirror Realm."

"And why would he want to do a thing like that?"

"Because the Queen of the Mirror Realm and my sister are *reflections*," Lacey tried to explain. But she knew she could not explain something that she could barely comprehend herself.

Turning, Tanner went to the door. He opened it, then looked back at Lacey. "I'll be back tomorrow with your uncle and we can all discuss it then."

"No! Wait!" Lacey said as Tanner left the room, closing the door behind him.

Outside, Tanner turned to the police officer who was guarding the door to Lacey's room. "I'll be back in the morning, Constable. Make sure Lacey Swift doesn't leave." Tanner then thrust his hands into his trouser pockets and walked away.

Chapter Twenty-Four

Abe and Marco had watched from the shadows of a nearby alleyway as Lacey had been carried into the ambulance on a stretcher. A man and a woman dressed in green-coloured overalls slammed the doors closed and went to the front of the vehicle. With sirens screeching and lights pulsating, the ambulance rushed away up Victoria Street pursued by several police officers on motorbikes.

"We'll have to follow that flashing thing," Marco said.

"I'm fast, but not that fast," Abe replied, staring at Marco with his bright red eyes.

"I can fly after it and then come back for you. Or I could fly with you in my arms..." Marco suggested.

"No thanks, no more flying for me," Abe said, sniffing the air with his long, white snout. "I have Lacey's scent. I can follow it."

"Are you sure?" Marco asked.

"Yes," Abe said. "Now get going."

Without another word, Marco rolled his shoulders beneath his coat, unfurling his wings. Tilting his head back, Marco rocketed up into the night sky.

Abe looked across the road at where the ambulance had been. He could see thin wispy tendrils of colour floating a few inches above the street. Just as he had seen Lacey through his spectacles in the Mirror Realm, he could now see his friend's scent, and it glowed a warm orange. Keeping to the shadows of shop doorways and the overhangs of tall buildings, Abe followed the orange wisps of colour along Victoria Street, past Westminster Cathedral, New Scotland Yard, the Houses of Parliament, and across Westminster Bridge until the tendrils of orange disappeared into a large building.

From a side alley, he heard his name being called and he looked to see Marco peeking out from behind several tall rubbish bins. Abe skulked into the alley and passed through hundreds of tendrils of mauve and black. These were bad scents; the smells of decaying waste and rotting food.

"They've taken Lacey into that big building. It's a hospital," Marco said as Abe came to a stop beside him.

"Is Lacey injured?" Abe asked.

"I don't know. I couldn't get too close, but she looked unconscious."

"Maybe one of those Night Hun... I mean *cops*, shot her?"

"No, I don't think so," Marco whispered in the darkness.

"How can you be so sure?"

"I would have been able to smell the blood. You don't get shot without losing some blood and believe me I would have smelt it." Marco breathed in then exhaled, releasing a plume of breath which floated away like a tiny cloud.

Abe eyed his friend and said, "Are you feeling okay?"

Marco nodded. "Just thirsty."

Abe had heard the tales of Blood Runners that had been through the mirrors. Most never returned as they had become addicts – addicted to the blood of humans. He knew that if Marco stayed for too long – if his thirst became too strong and he tasted human blood – just one little drop, Marco might never want to return home. He might not be able to.

"We're going to have to get Lacey out of there and back into the Mirror Realm as quickly as possible," Abe said, thinking aloud.

"What's the plan?" Marco asked.

"I don't know yet, but I'll think of something," Abe said, settling down and resting his snout on his giant paws.

"Well, think of something quick," Marco said, "I don't know what time sunrise is on this side of the mirrors, but I don't want to be here to find out."

Abe lay silent for the next few hours in the darkness of the alleyway, while Marco sat beside him, eyes closed. The wolf knew his friend wasn't sleeping. Abe could tell that Marco was meditating, trying to ignore his thirst, which grew more intense with every moment they stayed this side of the mirrors.

"How you doing?" Abe asked Marco after a few hours had passed.

"It feels like I've got an itch that I just can't reach and it's driving me mad," Marco said through clenched teeth. "How *you* doing?"

"What do you mean?" Abe asked.

"The plan! The plan!" Marco hissed, shivering now as if feverish.

Standing on all fours and peering across the street, Abe said, "Look who it is."

Marco opened his eyes and followed Abe's stare.

"I don't believe it," he whispered, watching Victor Swift climb from his car and skulk into the main entrance of St. Thomas's hospital.

"I have an idea. Follow me," Abe said, bounding across the street.

Chapter Twenty-Five

After being pointed in the right direction by the night porter, Victor Swift made his way through the labyrinth of corridors, passageways, and stairwells until he found his niece's room. He knew he had found the right place because only his obnoxious niece could command the presence of a police officer on guard outside her door.

Without making eye contact with the police officer, Victor went to enter Lacey's room. Before he had even managed to push the door open an inch, the police officer blocked his way with one muscular arm.

"Whoa, hang on a minute. You can't just go bowling in there. Who are you?" the police officer asked, eyeballing Victor.

Victor attempted a smile, but it looked more like a crack in a broken plate. "I'm Lacey's uncle," he said.

"I'll need to see some I.D." the police officer insisted, holding out his hand.

Sighing, Victor reached into his back trouser pocket and produced his wallet. He thumbed through it until he had found his driving license. Plucking it out, Victor thrust it under the nose of the police officer.

Without taking his eyes off Victor, the officer took the I.D. and said, "Thank you."

The officer then inspected the piece of plastic. He held it up and his eyes flicked between the photograph of Victor and the real thing that stood before him. Satisfying himself that he was the genuine article, the officer handed back the driving license.

"Is that all, officer?" Victor sneered.

"Yes," the officer said. "Everything seems to be in order."

"Then perhaps I could see my niece. She is sick, you know."

The officer motioned Victor toward the door without making further comment. Easing open the door, Victor slipped into the darkened room, closing the door behind him. He crossed the room in two lanky strides and stood beside his sleeping niece. Stooping, his spine gave an audible crack, as he leant over Lacey. Placing his puckered lips against her ear, Victor whispered, "*Laceeeey*, it's your Uncle Victor. I've come to take you home."

His whining voice penetrated Lacey's subconscious and she snapped open her eyes. Lacey's first thought on seeing her uncle's face leering over her was to scream. But before it had left her throat, Victor had placed one of his bony hands over her mouth.

"That's no way to greet your uncle," Victor said, his lips so thin and bloodless they looked as if all kindness had been bled from them.

Twisting beneath Victor's grip, Lacey thrashed her arms up and down.

"I can see that you're not going to come without a fight," Victor said.

Lacey recoiled under the vile warmth of her uncle's breath against her cheek. Reaching into his coat pocket with his free hand, Victor produced what appeared to be a thorn. Lacey's eyes widened as her uncle held it above her face. Whatever it was, it looked as if it had just been plucked from a rose bush. It was about an inch long, and its point was covered with a small metal cap. Removing the cap with his teeth, Victor spat it into the corner of the room. Then, holding the thorn between his thumb and forefinger, Victor brought it just millimetres from Lacey's face.

Lacey looked at the thorn's pointed tip and she could see a milky substance oozing from it.

"You don't need to be scared," Victor grinned. "Soon you'll be laughing about all of this."

Then with a surgeon's precision, Victor pushed the thorn into the side of Lacey's neck, burying it beneath her skin.

The Mirth-Barb, which Victor had elicited from his onetime lover, Araghney, took effect at once. Lacey began to chuckle. The chuckle then turned into laughter, which in turn became near hysterics. Placing one arm around Lacey's shoulders, Victor eased his niece from the bed.

"That's right, there's nothing to be scared of – not for the moment, anyhow. Now let's see if we can't get you dressed."

Victor helped his niece slide into her jeans and sweater as she fell about the room in fits of uncontrollable laughter. Tears streamed from her eyes and over her cheeks, and although to the outside world she appeared to be the happiest young woman on the planet, inside she was screaming: *"HELP ME! PLEASE SOMEBODY HELP ME!"*

But Lacey's lips just wouldn't let her form the words as she rolled around holding her sides. Once she was dressed, Victor looped his arm through Lacey's and used all of his strength to keep her from falling over. Victor pushed open the door and led Lacey into the corridor.

"Where do you think you're taking her?" the police officer said, stepping in front of Victor, barring his escape.

"I'm taking her home, to where she belongs," Victor said.

"I've had instructions not to let her leave," the police officer insisted as Victor tried to navigate his way around him.

"Is my niece under arrest?" Victor asked. "Has she been charged with some crime?"

The police officer shook his head. "Well, um… no… but…"

"Then as I understand the laws in this country, she is free to leave and you have no power to keep her here!" Victor spat.

"Look here," the police officer said, not knowing how to play this. However much he wanted to punch the smug idiot in the face, Victor did have a point. "Let me just seek advice on this."

"Seek advice?" Victor said. "Seek advice! Can't you see that she is delirious with happiness that I have come to fetch her home?"

Lacey looked at the police officer. Although she was giggling like a mindless fool, and wearing a grin that stretched from ear to ear, inside Lacey was yelling: *"PLEASE DON'T LET ME GO WITH HIM. HE'S GOING TO KILL ME!"*

The police officer looked at Lacey, who started giggling in front of him. She did seem happy enough in her uncle's company. *But what about Tanner?* the police officer reminded himself as those cold blue eyes of his superintendent bored into his mind.

"I'm going to have to call this one in," the police officer said. "I need to check this out with my super- "

"Do whatever you feel is necessary, officer, but I'm taking my niece home. You can contact me there if need be," Victor said, dragging his laughing niece up the corridor and out of the hospital.

The police officer just stood and watched as Victor disappeared. Deep down inside, he knew that he was going to be in a pile of shit. Someone was going to have to take the blame for this mess and crap ran downhill. The officer's hands moved to his equipment belt as he contemplated the situation. He then realised his handcuffs were missing, and that made him feel worse. That *was* down to him?

It was cold outside and the first rays of sunlight were beginning to break over the River Thames. Victor yanked open the rear passenger door of his car and threw Lacey face down onto the backseat. His niece found this amusing and sprayed a mouthful of laughter.

"See if you find this so funny," Victor said, taking the handcuffs he had slipped from the police officer's belt, snapping them around Lacey's wrists.

Victor slammed the car door shut and jumped into the driver's seat. He roared the engine into life and sped from the parking space and out onto the Embankment. Lacey roared with laughter and Victor screamed, *"Shut the fuck up! You're getting on my fucking nerves already!"*

Chapter Twenty-Six

Marco Lamia perched on top of St. Thomas's Hospital and trembled from head to toe. He gripped the stonework and his knuckles looked as if they were going to burst through the skin that covered his long fingers at any moment. The thirst was overwhelming now and he struggled to focus on the mission in hand. Marco was desperate to swoop from the sky and sink his teeth into the neck of one of those humans passing below on their way to work.

I could be down there and quench this thirst in seconds, he tried to convince himself. *But what if Victor should appear with Lacey while I was meant to be keeping watch? I might miss her and she would be left to her brutal uncle.* He knew that he and Lacey hadn't exactly hit it off – seen eye to eye – but all the same, he didn't want any harm to come to her. He needed her alive if he and his people were going to save their Queen and the Mirror Realm. But what was it that antagonized him so much about Lacey Swift? She was surely beautiful enough to rouse his interest. But he had been expecting something more from the one who he had risked so much to bring into the Mirror Realm – the one legend said would bring peace to his world. Perhaps there had been a mistake? Perhaps she wasn't the one. Not all myths and legends turned out to be correct. But if he were to be brutally honest, he was infuriated with himself that there was something about her that he found so attractive. It wasn't just her prettiness, the way the leather trousers and coat clung to her figure that stirred feelings within him, there was something else, too. But he didn't know what.

Pushing thoughts of Lacey from his mind, Marco fought the temptations that his thirst conjured in his mind. But the thirst for human blood that he felt on this side of the mirrors wasn't the sole reason he felt so feverish. The sun was rising, spraying its rays like a pink halo across the river. His flesh itched and had started to feel sore. Marco knew it wouldn't be long before his skin started to blister, crack, and wither.

Abe had told him not to strike until Victor had left the city and was well away from people. "Wait until we reach a quiet road. Somewhere nice and secluded," Abe had stressed.

But that had been over an hour ago and it had still been pitch-black. Marco had no intention of being burnt to a cinder, so he had altered the plan. He had decided that as soon as

Victor appeared, he was going to strike. Closing his eyes, Marco fought the temptation to swoop down and quench his thirst. He rocked, semi-conscious, on the lip of the hospital building and trembled. Without realising, he had begun to lose his grip, teetering ever nearer to the edge. Then, as Marco was about to fall, he snapped open his eyes and tightened his grip. He looked down at all those passing humans with that gorgeous warm red stuff pumping through them. Crying out as if in pain, his lips rolled back revealing a gaping red mouth, which was full of razor-sharp teeth. Marco trembled, his eyes as black as two pits. In his mind's eye, he could see himself lunging down at one of the passing humans, ripping their throat out. Marco could almost smell and taste the warm red liquid gushing into his mouth and down his throat.

One kill wouldn't hurt, would it? he wondered. *I'm so thirsty – I can't bear it – it's driving me insane. Just a mouthful – that would do. Just one mouthful!*

Snapping open his eyes, teeth gleaming in the light of the dawn, Marco readied himself to swoop down and take one of the humans when he saw Victor's car speeding away from the parking space outside the hospital and go racing along the embankment.

Without hesitating, Marco let go of his

perch and dropped through the sky like a stone. He raced toward the ground below and, just when it looked as if he was going to smash head-first into the pavement, Marco shook his shoulders, letting his dead-black wings unfold. He soared over the bridge as he sped after Victor's car.

With his wings rippling like kites on either side of him, Marco flew level with the car and peered inside. He could see Lacey lying face down on the backseat, her wrists bound. That was part 'A' of the plan accomplished. Abe had told him that there was no point in striking if Victor had been unsuccessful in taking Lacey from the hospital.

"Now for part 'B'," Marco muttered to himself through gritted teeth. He shot forward at great speed, racing ahead of the car. Arcing through the air, Marco turned so he was facing the vehicle and went flying toward it.

Victor was still screaming at Lacey to stop laughing when Marco hit the windscreen like a rocket. Victor looked up to see Marco's fangs inches from his face on the other side of the windshield, which was cracked like a sprawling spider's web. The vampire that now sat perched on the front of the car bonnet, wings spread open, made it impossible for Victor to see the road that lay ahead. Covering his face with his hands, Victor lost control of the car. It went careering across the path of oncoming traffic. Taxis spun three-hundred-and-sixty degrees to avoid the car. Buses skidded on the icy roads and crunched into one another, sending passengers screaming for the emergency exits.

It was too early in the day for tourists, but those commuters making their way to the tube stations to get to work produced mobile phones and began recording their latest upload to their social media accounts. Yet, even they couldn't have imagined what was going to happen next.

Victor's car nosedived into the embankment wall that ran parallel with the River Thames. The front of the car crumpled as if made from tissue. Marco shot from the hood and cart-wheeled through the air. Arching his back, the wings grew taut and he broke his fall, hovering just above the car. Victor sat dazed and confused in the driver's seat. He rubbed his nose, which was now gushing blood down the front of his clothes. The coppery scent of it wafted on the air, causing Marco's stomach to somersault with hunger. The impact of the crash had thrown Lacey from the backseat and into the foot-well between the front and back seats. But still she roared with uncontrollable laughter. Even as the boot of the car exploded open, Lacey laughed.

Hundreds of people were now gathered

on the streets and roads along the embankment that led to the London Eye. As they watched and filmed in amazement, two giant paws burst out of the boot of the car, tearing it open as if it were made of papier-mâché. The sound of metal being torn was followed by a deep, throaty growl, which made the spectators' chests rattle as if they were standing too close to a speaker playing the bass at full blast. The boot of the car flew through the air, spinning away like a Frisbee. Some of the onlookers ducked out of its way as it spun over the river. Others began to scream as the biggest wolf they had ever seen sprang from the boot of the car and landed on top of the vehicle. In the distance the sounds of sirens could be heard as the police raced toward the scene.

Abe stood on top of the car and the roof began to crumble inwards under his weight. Arching his back, he roared into the morning sun and howled. Making a fist with his right paw, Abe punched it through the roof of the car and tore it open like a can of sardines. He reached in and pulled Lacey out.

The spectators screamed and wailed as the giant wolf, using his jaws, pulled Lacey from within the wrecked innards of the car.

"Look! The wolf is going to kill her!" one woman said at the top of her voice.

"Somebody do something!" a male shouted, gesturing toward the wolf with his umbrella.

"Hang on!" someone else shouted from nearby. "The young woman thinks it's funny. Look, she's laughing!"

Seeing this, those who hadn't already begun to film this peculiar incident searched for their phones in their handbags or pockets. They too wanted an exclusive they could later sell to the highest bidder. But when each of them glanced down at their phones, or checked the footage later, all they found they had recorded was a series of twisting streams of bright white light. Somehow, all of them had failed to get footage or even a photograph of the wolf, vampire, and the laughing girl.

Without warning, Abe threw Lacey into the air. She tumbled upwards and, just as she reached the peak of her ascent, Marco swooped down and snatched her out of the air. He soared upwards as he fought to hold onto Lacey, who was still laughing hysterically. The sun was almost up now and Marco's exposed skin had begun to smoke beneath its rays. His whole being trembled as if he were freezing cold, yet his skin was seething with heat. Fearing that he may lose his grip on Lacey, Marco corkscrewed up through the air and came to rest on one of the giant glass pods attached to the giant Ferris wheel, the London Eye.

Abe looked upwards and, seeing his friend's precarious position on the colossal Ferris wheel, he glanced back into the car in search of Victor Swift. To his dismay the driver's seat was empty. Victor had fled.

The sirens were close now and Abe knew that those Night Hunters – cops – wouldn't let him and his friends escape again. Leaping from the crumpled and twisted heap of metal that was Victor's car, Abe bounded along the embankment, howling and barking at the crowds that had gathered. As he drew near to the London Eye, he leapt through the air, and unleashing his claws, he began to climb the metal struts to the top.

Marco held onto Lacey as she continued to wriggle and laugh against him. Marco was burning up now and his thirst was driving him to the edge of his own sanity. Maybe if he had something to drink, something to cool his throat, perhaps he wouldn't feel so bad. He held Lacey in his arms and looked down at her neck. He then leant forward, and placing his lips about Lacey's throat, he began to suck.

"Marco, stop!" Abe howled, reaching them.

Marco's lips had formed a vacuum around

Lacey's neck, and Abe could see the muscles in his friend's throat pumping up and down as he drank.

"Let go of Lacey!" Abe barked, swiping at Marco with a huge paw.

Marco broke the seal his lips had formed around Lacey's neck and looked at Abe. "Do you think I would kill our friend?"

"What were you doing if you weren't drinking her blood?" Abe snarled.

Marco opened his hand and spat something into his open palm. Abe looked down and could see what looked like a thorn lying in the creases of his smouldering flesh.

"What's that?" Abe asked.

"Poison," Marco said, cradling Lacey to his chest. Now that he had plucked the poisonous thorn from her neck, Lacey was still and breathing heavily as if catching her breath.

Abe looked down at the streets below and at all the upturned faces, blue flashing lights and police officers. "How do we get out of this alive?"

"Through that mirror," Lacey said, peering over the crook of Marco's elbow.

Abe and Marco looked up. Floating in the air just feet from them was a long, narrow and gleaming mirror. The three friends could see themselves reflected in it. But behind them wasn't the sun breaking over the Thames and sparkling off the many glass pods attached to the London Eye, but a star-shot night sky.

Shaking all over, Marco stood on the large glass pod he and his friends were perched on. Holding Lacey in his arms, he said, "Let's go home."

He then flew into the mirror as Abe leapt through after him.

They tumbled through the air as the mirror shattered above, spraying the night with a thousand more pieces of sparkling shards. Marco, Lacey, and Abe seemed to fall forever, the wind rushing past them, pulling at their hair and clothes. Even if Marco still had his wings they wouldn't have saved him. Marco was unconscious, his pale skin smouldering like burning wax.

With a terrifying splash they hit water, disappearing beneath the thick, black waves of the Onyx Sea.

Chapter Twenty-Seven

Tanner sat forward at his office desk on the third floor at New Scotland Yard, when his airwave radio started to spew frantic messages about a huge wolf on the rampage near the London Eye. Pulling the radio from its charger, Tanner stood up. Pacing the room, he pressed the radio to his ear.

"Alpha-Bravo-two-seven to control. We need urgent assistance at the London Eye. We have a re-sighting of the hostiles."

"Where's the young woman, Lacey Swift?" Tanner said into the radio.

The cop on the ground didn't need to be reminded of Tanner's call-sign to know it was him transmitting over the airwaves. Everyone and anyone who policed this part of London recognised his unmistakable, dry tone.

"The hostiles have her, sir," came the police officer's reply.

Realising that the officer who had been instructed to guard Lacey Swift at the hospital had either fallen asleep on the job or gotten lazy infuriated Tanner, and he rubbed the bridge of his nose. Now wasn't the time for Tanner to chase this officer for a duty report. He would deal with him later. It didn't matter what excuses the constable gave for this oversight; he would be spending the next six months washing out the filthiest cells in the most antiquated custody block in London he could find.

Tanner turned the volume knob of his radio to maximum and strained to make sense of the garbled, incoherent messages of the police officers on the ground.

"The bat's on one of the pods!" an officer reported down the radio.

"It's got the young woman! The bat-thing has got Lacey Swift!" another one roared through the radio.

"The wolf's climbing up the side of the London Eye!" a static-sounding voice said.

Tanner snapped the radio onto his belt and pulled his coat from the stand in the corner of his office. It sounded as if the drama that was unfolding along the South Bank of the River Thames could turn into a hostage situation, and Tanner wanted to be there to take command from the very start. Without any direction from his senior officers, this was going to be his case and his case alone.

Just as Tanner was about to leave his office, a confused and startled voice blurted over off the radio: "A mirror has just appeared in the sky! Can somebody else confirm that a mirror has just appeared in the sky?"

"Roger that, two-four," came the voice of another confused and bewildered officer. "I can also see the mirror."

Tanner froze. The word *'mirror'* rang in his ears and his heart began to race. He crossed back to his desk and sat down, steepling his fingers under his chin. He closed his icy-blue eyes.

"The hostiles have disappeared!" a cop yelled over the airwaves.

Tanner snatched the radio from his belt and breathed into it. "What about the girl? Where is Lacey Swift?"

There was a hiss of static and then one brave officer updated their superintendent by saying in a breathless voice, "We have lost the girl... we have lost Lacey Swift."

"Where did she go?" Tanner asked.

Again there was silence, but this time it lasted longer. Then the police officer's voice broke over the radio and said, "She went through the mirror, sir. I can confirm she disappeared into the mirror."

Tanner placed the radio in the centre of his desk. Keeping his eyes closed, he began to rub the bridge of his nose again. In his mind's eye he pictured the mirror. It stood before him, just out of reach. He stuck out his hand, gliding his fingertips over its cool, smooth surface. In his mind's eye, he could see himself reflected back in it. Tanner opened his eyes and smiled. Hovering in the centre of his office, just on the other side of his desk, was *his* mirror. He smoothed his moustache with one strong hand and stood. He approached the mirror that rippled before him as if caught in a breeze. Without hesitating, Tanner stepped into the mirror.

It was good to be back, he thought to himself as he stood and looked out of the window of the office and along the deserted street that wound its way through the town of Dawn Wall. Dec Tanner glanced over his shoulder as the mirror cracked, splintered, and fell to the floor in a series of glittering shards.

Tanner pulled up the hood of the long, dark coat he now wore, over his white wiry hair. He tightened the holsters that crisscrossed his waist. Opening the door, he stepped out onto the cobblestoned street that twisted away to his left and right. A wet mist hung in the air, and the wind was cold. Pulling the collar up of his long, black coat, Tanner turned and closed the door of the office – the place where the other Night Hunters like him had once worked from. The humans on the other side of the mirrors would have called it a police station. Once the door was shut tight, Tanner made his way along the winding street.

The heels of his boots echoed off the cobbles and the ancient stone buildings that stood empty on either side of him. The crossbows strapped about his waist thumped heavily against each thigh. Halfway down the street, Tanner stopped and turned to face a door. The blue paint that once covered it was peeling away in strips, revealing the wood beneath. He pushed the door open and strode into the *Screaming Jackal* pub.

His blue eyes surveyed the empty bar. He could remember a time when it would have been bristling with life. The men-folk from the town propped against the bar as they supped jugs of beer. Women and men dancing together to music being played on the ancient piano in the corner. All that had changed now. All of them taken prisoner or cursed. Their businesses and farms destroyed by Draconia. Although they were all gone now, Tanner could still hear their music and the sounds of their laughter. It seemed to have permeated the air like a wine stain on a white-coloured tablecloth.

He looked across the bar and up at the landing that ran around the upper level of the pub. He stared at the many doors that led from it.

His eyes burnt as he remembered her standing there outside the room they had shared. They were to be married, but Meadda had long since left the town of Dawn Wall. She had done so for her own safety. But Tanner hadn't seen her since that day and doubted he ever would see her again, however much his heart longed for her.

Gritting his teeth, he turned, and pushing a table out of his way, he went to the far corner of the pub where the piano had once been played. He looked back over his shoulder just to make sure that he wasn't being watched. Tanner did this more out of habit than need, as there was just the seven of them hiding out in Dawn Wall and he hadn't seen anyone pass this way in months. Confident that he wasn't being spied on, Tanner pulled away a panel that was secreted into the wall. Brushing away a veil of cobwebs, he placed his mouth up against the opening and whispered into the darkness, "Hey! You down there! Get your kit together. Our wait is over. I believe it's started to happen."

Chapter Twenty-Eight

As Tanner stepped into the Mirror Realm, Victor slithered up against the remains of his car. He watched the police officers race back and forth, not one of them the faintest idea as to what had happened and what to do about it. Victor arched his back and rubbed at his temples.

"My mirror. I must be able to see my mirror," he whined.

Closing his eyes, he tried to picture his mirror. But there was just too much noise. Those blasted sirens approaching from the distance were distracting him. He needed a certain amount of tranquillity if he was to conjure his mirror and escape into the world beyond it. Victor needed his most favourite chair and he needed the warmth of the fireplace.

"I need some goddamn peace and quiet!" he screeched at no-one in particular, rolling his hands into fists and slamming them against the road like a spoilt child.

Closing his eyes again, he fought to block out the distractions that were all around him. Then, in the darkness of his mind, he could see it. The mirror stood at the end of a long corridor that bored its way into the deepest and darkest part of his mind. He staggered toward it like a man dying of thirst and could see a stream in the distance.

"Come closer!" he screeched, as police cars, ambulances, and fire trucks arrived on scene.

"Come closer," he begged again. *"I need to be away from here!"*

Inside his mind, he reached for the mirror that almost seemed to beckon him forward. Victor placed his bony hands over his ears and screwed up his eyes as he fought to concentrate on the mirror.

"Don't you disappear on me now!" he roared at if it were a living thing.

"Hey, look at that man," someone in the crowd shouted. "What's he doing?"

Hearing this, some of the other spectators turned to watch Victor as he staggered around in the middle of the chaos, eyes closed, arms outstretched, hands clutching for something that only he could see.

"What's his problem?" someone yelled.

Inside his head, Victor had reached his mirror. He clung to the edges of it. But he couldn't step through – into it – and the world beyond. There was still too much noise for him to fully concentrate and bleed into the gleaming surface.

"Let me through! Let me in!"

Screaming, Victor fell through the mirror. Passing between the realms had never hurt before. In fact, he had found it exhilarating, almost addictive, but this time around it had been agony. Victor lay in the sand and gasped for breath. He felt as if he had been turned inside out. He frantically patted himself just to make sure that his lungs, heart and intestines weren't hanging from his coat.

Why am I in so much pain? he wondered, thrusting one skinny hand into his mouth to stop himself from throwing up.

Perhaps it was because the mirror wasn't complete before me? he guessed. Victor realised that if he were to avoid such an agonising experience again, he would have to work on, and master, conjuring his mirror in quick time and in whatever circumstance he happened to find himself in.

Things had started to go from bad to worse, and he knew deep in his black heart that he was losing control over events. He couldn't rely on being in the comfortable surroundings of his cottage if he was to pass into the Mirror Realm. He might need to do it anywhere now. He might have to conjure the mirror while on the run.

But what should I do now? he thought, his

head pounding again.

"Stop it!" he hissed, tapping his temples with the tips of his fingers. "Don't you dare start thumping." He wondered whether he should go straight to Draconia. But what would Victor tell him about the mess that had unravelled on the other side of the mirrors. Victor ran the back of his hand across his brow. He felt hot beneath the sun that was rising above him. His thoughts turned to Thea, and he knew that he needed to go back through the mirrors and give her some more of those pills. But should he go back now – so soon – or head to the Splinter and Draconia? Then, he saw something that made up his mind for him.

Crouching on all fours, Victor hid himself behind some rocks that jutted from the sand. He spied over the top of them. He licked the taste of sea salt from his lips as he watched Lacey and her friends fighting for their lives in the murky waves that rushed the shore below.

Chapter Twenty-Nine

Lacey kicked her legs against the water, but it felt thick and gloopy, like slush. With her hands cuffed behind her back, she struggled to keep her head above the waves. The water took Lacey again, forcing her head under and smothering her. The waves were so black that Lacey found it almost impossible to see anything beneath the sea. She kicked her legs again as the sea squirted into her mouth, up her nostrils and down her throat. Her head bobbed above sea level again and she coughed the fluid from her lungs like dark lumps of phlegm.

Lacey looked around and could see the shoreline in the distance, but with her arms restrained in the small of her back and the heavy water clinging to her like wet sand, she knew it would be impossible for her to reach the safety of the beach. Again Lacey went under the water, and she struggled to draw breath as her head sunk beneath the surface. She could feel her lungs becoming heavy and the thought of just closing her eyes and going to sleep seemed overwhelming. Like a stone, Lacey began to plunge deeper and deeper beneath the waves. Just as she closed her eyes and could feel sleep taking her to the bottom of the sea, something coiled itself around her waist, dragging her back to the surface.

Gasping and choking like an old car trying to start on a freezing cold morning, Lacey sucked mouthfuls of sea air into her lungs. She thrashed her legs and somebody shouted in her ear, "Stop struggling, Lacey. I'm trying to save you!"

Although Lacey had thick, black waves sloshing around her ears, she recognised that voice at once.

"Abe," she coughed. "Where's Marco?"

"I've already got him onto the shore, but he won't survive for long under this blistering sun. So stop flapping and help me!" Abe cried.

Trying to relax every muscle in her body, Lacey lay back in her friend's arms as Abe swam back to the shore. As soon as Lacey could feel the seabed beneath her feet, Abe released his grip on his friend and Lacey stumbled up the beach, collapsing onto her side in the sand.

"We don't have time to lay around," Abe yelled. "We've got to get Marco into some kind of shelter and out of the sun." He bounded toward Lacey. Pulling one of the crossbows from his friend's holster, Abe spun Lacey over in the sand and ordered her to raise her arms behind her back. Taking aim, Abe pointed the crossbow at the links of metal that joined the cuffs about

Lacey's gloved wrists.

Lacey lifted her face out of the sand and looked back over her shoulder. Seeing Abe there, his large eyes hidden behind those thick black lenses again, and pointing the crossbow at her, she cried out, "Hang on a minute, are you sure your eyesight is..."

Before Lacey had finished shouting her warning, the air vibrated with an ear-splitting boom as Abe fired the crossbow, tearing apart the handcuffs. Feeling the cuffs disintegrate, Lacey pulled her arms free and rubbed her aching wrists. She could see that she was once more wearing the leather gauntlet that covered her left forearm. The knives and blades that covered it gleamed in the sunlight. The circular copper housing, with the hole at its centre, was still attached to it. The jagged scar that covered her wrist beneath the gauntlet throbbed like a dull toothache. Abe threw the crossbow into the sand and turned his attention to Marco.

Still choking up stringy lumps of black mucus, Lacey rolled onto her side and watched Abe wrap Marco in his cloak. Abe was back to his former self – more human-looking than that of a wolf. He was dressed in his brown rough-looking shirt and blue trousers. As before, his feet were bare and he wore those dark glasses. Abe threw the supplies that his father had left over his shoulder, then swooped Marco up into his arms. He then charged up the beach toward a severe-looking cliff-face that loomed in the distance.

Lacey rolled onto her knees then forced herself up onto her feet. She stood and brushed sand from her wet clothes that Abe had given to her in the forest. The gun belt hung about her waist, and once more, the crossbows were tethered about each thigh. She fastened the front of the coat with the fishhook shaped clasps and pulled the hood of her coat up over her head. Dressed like a Night Hunter once more, she gathered together the supplies that Abe's father, Fletcher, had previously given to them. She then made her way along the beach after Abe.

A large overhang of rock that jutted out like a boxer's chin offered plenty of cool shadows for Marco to rest in. Laying him on the ground, Abe peeled back Marco's cloak like a nurse removing a bandage from a wound. Marco appeared to be unconscious and wafts of smoke curled upwards from his skin, which looked blistered and sore. Lacey gazed down at Marco's scorched and peeling face. She knew that for the second time since their meeting, Marco had risked his own life to save hers. He had risked being burnt to death in the desert as he had searched for her mirror, and now again, on the other side of mirrors trying to rescue her from

Victor's clutches.

"Will he be okay?' Lacey whispered, not wanting to disturb him.

Abe looked at her from behind his black lenses and shrugged. "I don't know. He was out in the sun for longer than I've known before. Marco's skin looks pretty raw. Time will tell, I guess. All we can do is wait."

Abe slumped down in the shade and pulled some of the raw rabbit meat, provided by his father, from his bag. He unfolded the leaves that it had been wrapped in and began gnawing on it. Lacey sat opposite him and rubbed her wrists and inspected the gauntlet with the knives and daggers. She ran her gloved fingers over the copper-coloured housing fixed to it. She wondered what it was for. The throbbing pain she had felt from the scar had eased.

"Aren't you going to eat?" Abe mumbled, swirling the meat around the inside of his mouth.

"I'd prefer mine cooked instead of raw," Lacey grimaced as Abe smacked his lips together and then licked his fingers clean.

"I could always get a fire going," Abe suggested. "There's plenty of driftwood lying around down on the beach, washed up from shipwrecks."

Watching Abe pick stringy pieces of meat from between his sharp teeth, Lacey shook her head and said, "Don't worry about it for now. I'm not hungry. I'll eat later."

They sat without speaking and listened to the sound of the thick, black waves crashing against the beach. Lacey eventually broke the silence and said, "Well, we're back where we started, I guess."

"What do you mean?" Abe asked.

"We're back on the beach, where we stepped through the mirror," Lacey sighed, looking out across the black choppy waves. "We have no way of crossing the sea to get to the prison you spoke of and the prisoner…"

"We've crossed the Onyx Sea," Abe said.

"How can you be so sure?"

Pointing one long finger into the distance, Abe said, "See those four big shadows in the distance?"

Lacey looked in the direction that Abe was pointing. Way off in the distance, four enormous towers soared up into the sky like giants trying to reach out and touch the clouds.

"They're the search towers that surround Bleakstorm Prison."

"I thought you said that it was built below ground?" Lacey said, staring into the distance at the daunting towers.

"I said the prisoners were kept underground," Abe said, his eyes glowing bright behind his glasses.

"So who's this prisoner?' Lacey asked, as Marco murmured in his sleep where he lay in the corner of the overhang.

"The prisoner has the key," Abe reminded her.

"I know that," Lacey said. "But who is he?"

Abe placed the leaves on the ground beside him and folded his arms over his knees, which he had drawn up beneath his chin. "The prisoner is my grandfather," Abe said.

"Really?" Lacey gasped. "What did he do to get himself sent to prison?"

"Nothing," Abe said, without looking up. "He got sent there because of me."

"Because of you?" Lacey frowned. "What did you do?"

"I opened the box," Abe said.

Lacey sat and shook her head. "But I don't understand, Abe. Why would opening that box get your grandfather thrown into prison?"

Abe raised his head and stared into Lacey's eyes. "Because if I hadn't opened it, none of this would've happened."

"None of what?"

"Everything," Abe said. "If I had done as my father had instructed, then we wouldn't be sitting here right now having this conversation. My father wouldn't be blind, the Mirror Realm wouldn't be getting eaten by the desert, Marco's people wouldn't have been cursed, the wolves wouldn't have fled to the Snowstorm Mountains, and your sister and my Queen wouldn't be dying."

Lacey sat and tried to comprehend what it was that Abe had told her. "I can't believe that you could be responsible for everything that has gone bad in our two worlds. It doesn't seem fair. It doesn't seem possible."

"I'll tell you what I did. Then you'll see why *I* had to come and find the key if I am to stand any chance of putting right everything that has gone so wrong. But more than anything, I want to hear my father say that he forgives me," Abe said.

Chapter Thirty

The blistering sun sat at its highest point above the Onyx Sea and its rays sparkled on the waves like glitter. Abe rolled Marco to the furthest corner of the rocky overhang and tightened the cloak about him. Content that his friend was well covered from the light of the sun, Abe slumped against the rocky wall and looked at Lacey through his thick, black lenses. Although Abe was tall and muscular, he now looked smaller somehow, as if he were drawing in on himself.

"My father was an ironsmith by trade. The best in the whole of the Mirror Realm. His father was one before him, and it was hoped that one day I would follow them both into the family business," Abe began to explain. "On the same day every year, the Queen would summon my father and grandfather to the Splinter. Knowing how skilled a craftsman they were, she entrusted them to repair the seals on the box that contained the Click – the shard of broken mirror I told you about," he said, glancing up at Lacey who sat against the wall on the opposite side of the overhang.

"Why did the seals need to be repaired?" Lacey asked, spinning the chamber of one of her crossbows with her thumb.

"That box might contain just a single piece of broken mirror, but one thing's for sure, it's powerful and after a time it erodes the box. The Queen was fearful that its power may escape from it. So, once a year, if it needed repairing or not, my father and grandfather would be entrusted to check its seals and carry out any repairs. My grandfather was also a gifted locksmith, and it would be his task to cut a new key and lock for the box. There was only ever to be the one key, the Queen forbade a second to be made."

Holstering her crossbow, Lacey looked across the overhang at Abe and said, "So where do you fit into all of this?"

"I shouldn't have been a part of this at all," Abe said, looking down at his claw-like hands clasped in his lap. "Just my father and grandfather were trusted to enter the Splinter and work on the box. But every year I pleaded with my father to take me with him, and every year, keeping his promise to the Queen, he refused. So one year, I snuck aboard my father's stagecoach, and without him knowing, I went to the Splinter.

"I can remember how hungry I had

become whilst hiding under the pile of rough sacks in the rear of the carriage for the three days and nights it had taken to cross the wastelands to the Splinter. I had hidden there as the smell of roasted meat had wafted from the campfire my father had made. On the second night, my stomach had growled so loud with hunger, I feared my father and grandfather would discover me.

"I lay beneath the sacks and wiped the saliva from my mouth with the back of my hands. Screwing my eyes shut, I imagined what could be inside the box that my family had been entrusted to repair for so many years. I remembered how on my father's return from previous trips I had hung around his giant legs and begged to know what was inside.

"'Please, father, tell me, what's inside the box?'

"Ruffling up my hair with his huge hands, my father would look down at me with his big, brown eyes and smile. 'A Click... or so they say.'

"'But what does it *look* like?' I would howl.

"'Neither I nor your grandfather get to open the box, the Queen forbids it. I mend the box's seals and your grandfather fits a new lock and key. Then we come home and forget all about it.'

"'But don't you want to see inside the

box?' I would pester. 'Don't you want to see what the Click looks like?'

"My father would hunker down so he was at my height and look into my pale green eyes. 'Sometimes in life, you don't always get to find out what's inside the box. Just like you don't always get the answers to all of your questions.'

"Then, saying not another word about it, my father would get up and unpack the stagecoach.

"I lay in the dark at the back of the carriage and dreamed of what that Click looked like," Abe continued to explain. "On the third day, the Stagecoach began to slow, and poking my head from beneath the sacks, I peered through the coach's windows as it passed through the enormous gates of the Splinter. The gates towered so far into the sky that I lost sight of them amongst the clouds. The Splinter was surrounded by a complex maze of white cobbled streets, which were lined with a thousand different kinds of shops, selling everything from the most delicious-looking sweets to succulent loins of meat. I was amazed to discover that there appeared to be a secret city built behind the gates of the Splinter.

"My father and grandfather guided the stagecoach deeper into this city and toward the Splinter itself. We passed a thriving market where traders sold mouth-watering looking fruit, plants, animals, and medicines. There were street-side conjurers, dancers, and bands playing the sweetest of music. I stared wide-eyed from my hiding place, and got the overwhelming feeling that the Splinter was a happy place – a place of peace and tranquillity.

"My father steered the stagecoach away from the main plaza and up a long, winding strip to the rear of the Splinter. The vehicle came to a halt outside a large set of wooden doors. I listened from the dark as someone approached the stagecoach.

"'Has it been a year already since I last saw you?' a voice asked.

"Pressing one eye to a gap in the carriage window, I saw a tall, lean man standing and looking up at my father and grandfather. This man wore a silver-plated helmet that had spikes protruding from it where his ears would have been hidden underneath. Jutting down from the brow of the helmet was a metal nosepiece, which gave the appearance that the man was wearing some type of mask. He wore a sliver chest-plate that had a red cross painted across its centre. Metal gauntlets covered his wrists, and from these hung long lengths of red ribbon and as they twisted in the breeze it looked like his wrist had been cut and he was bleeding. Beneath the armour he wore a white tunic that hung low over his legs, and he wore boots that were covered in gleaming chainmail. A scabbard hung from his waist and housed a long, razor-sharp sword. Over his back was thrown a silver shield. From the way this man was dressed, I could see that he was a Splinter Knight.

"'The years pass quickly, Sir Isake,' my father replied, sticking out one giant hand.

"With my eye pressed to the gap in the stagecoach door, I watched the Splinter Knight, Sir Isake, reach out and take what appeared to be a piece of parchment paper from my father. Unrolling it, the knight squinted at the paper from beneath the thick brow of the helmet he wore.

"'This seems to be all in order. Signed in her majesty's own hand,' Sir Isake said, handing back the signed letter of authority that gave my father and grandfather access to the box.

"Sir Isake's armour and helmet blazed in the mid-morning sun as he made his way to the double set of doors and forced them open. The stagecoach rolled forward on its giant wheels and entered the Splinter.

"'Do you not want to search the carriage?' I heard my grandfather ask.

"Hearing this, my heart began to race and I buried myself beneath the rough woven sacks.

"'You have been coming here on the same day for more years than I can care to remember and you've never so much as caused me a problem. There is not a more trustworthy race than yours in the whole of the Mirror Realm. I don't need to search your carriage,' Sir Isake said, to my utter relief.

"'Thank you, Sir Isake. We will be just a few hours,' my father said, steering the carriage inside the Splinter.

"'I'll be just outside the door should you need anything,' Sir Isake said, sliding the doors shut and standing guard outside.

"From my hiding place, I could hear my father and grandfather climb from the stagecoach. The horses that had pulled them, and me in secret, all the way from the Howling Forests kicked at the cobbled floor of the workshop with their hooves. From my hiding place, I watched my grandfather stroke their long, black manes and they neighed with contentment.

"My father went to the middle of the workshop and there, just like it had been left for him so many times before, sat the box. It had been placed on a small wooden table which was littered with candles that glowed within tall glass vases. With reverence, my father removed the plain linen cloth that had been placed over it. He looked down at the box and stroked his long, brown beard.

"'The work we carried out last year seems to have held,' he said, glancing round at my grandfather.

"He shuffled toward the table, his greying hair hanging in wispy lengths from his head, face, and hands. My grandfather eyed the box without touching it.

"'That it does,' he said. 'Best check it again, just to make sure.'

"My father disappeared into the shadows of the workshop and returned with a box of odd-looking tools. My grandfather picked up a key that had been left next to the box on the table and held it before him. I peered from the darkness of the carriage at the key that dangled from a chain in the shimmering candlelight.

"To my disappointment the key looked very ordinary. I had been expecting something more intricate, more cunning in its design than the two-teethed key my grandfather held in his claw.

"'Remove the lock and I shall make a start on the box,' my father said.

"Stooping over the table, and with a trembling hand, my grandfather placed the key into the lock. He twisted it several times, up and down and from left to right. There was a gentle hissing sound as if the lock were releasing a jet of steam. It snapped open. My grandfather removed the lock and the unbreakable chain that encompassed the box.

"Away from the table, in the opposite corner of the room to where the stagecoach was parked, stood a vat of what looked like boiling molten lava. I continued to spy as my grandfather threw the lock and the key into the vat, destroying them both forever. Without saying a word, my grandfather shuffled to a nearby workbench and set about making a new lock and key for the box.

"For what seemed like an eternity, my father and grandfather worked in silence as they carried out their repairs. I watched, absorbing everything that they did. It was while I sat in the dark and spied on them that the box seemed to call to me. Not in words but in *feelings*. For every moment that I sat hidden in the dark, I felt the urge to leap from my hiding place and throw open the lid. The need to do so became unbearable. The longer I stayed hidden, the more my eyes were drawn to the box, and the longer my eyes looked at the box, the harder it became to tear them away from it. Something else was happening to me, too. It wasn't just that I was unable to take my gaze from the box, my feelings toward my father and grandfather began to change.

'"Why should they be entrusted to touch the box?' I seethed, under my breath. 'What makes them so special?'

"I watched my father turn the box in his giant hands and I became consumed with jealousy.

'"Look at him holding it! If he can touch it, then why shouldn't I?' I hissed in the dark.

"I watched my grandfather go to the box and hold the new lock that he had made against it to make sure that it was a perfect fit.

'"Look at that stupid old fool,' I spat. 'That box isn't meant to be locked. It should be open for all to see inside.'

"From my hiding place, I waited for my grandfather and father to move away from the box, as when they did, I had decided I was going to open it. With my heart racing in my chest, I pulled down on the handle of the carriage door and waited to pounce. With my eyes fixed on the box, I flung open the carriage door and lunged across the workshop. Grinning like I was insane, I snatched up the box, cradling it to my chest. Then, without any hesitation, I wrenched open the lid." Abe said, staring at Lacey.

Chapter Thirty-One

Lacey looked at Abe, who sat on the opposite side of the overhang. His story had so engrossed her that she had not noticed the tide creep up the shore, and it broke against the grey sand just feet away now. The sky was darker, as the sun crept down and the moon readied to put in an appearance within an hour or two.

This was the first time since meeting her strange new friend – the person responsible for pulling her into the Mirror Realm – that he had truly said anything about himself or explained his past. From what Abe had said so far, Lacey now had the distinct impression that Abe's past was closely aligned to the events that were now unravelling about them.

Keen to know more, Lacey leant forward and said, "So what happened when you opened the box?"

Abe drew his knees up to his chest, long claws hanging over them. He took a deep breath, then said, "I looked into the box, and at first I was disappointed. All that was in the box was a shard of mirror. But gradually, I became delighted and enthralled. My face became a mask of pleasure as

I looked upon that piece of broken mirror.

"'It's beautiful!' I howled. *'It's sooo beautiful!'*

"Hearing my voice, my father spun round to find me standing in the middle of the workshop with the box open. Light blazed from within the box and I looked as if I had been sprayed with moonlight.

"'*No, you fool!*' my father roared, bounding toward me.

"But I continued to stare transfixed at the beautiful vision inside the box. Then something changed. Something within the box scared me and I began to shake with fear. So terrified did I become, that I began to scream until my throat was raw. The light from the box no longer looked cool like moonlight, but intense and scorching like the rays from a hot sun. I felt my eyes begin to grow warm in their sockets then start to boil as if on fire. My pupils began to smoulder as flames licked from my tear ducts. The spell, if that's what it had been, was broken. The box had been snatched from me. I fell to the rough floor of the workshop. My father held the box which he had taken from me. The light poured from it like a fountain that was flowing uphill. It splashed his face, and just like I had moments before, he became mesmerised by it.

"My father stared into the box and

screamed. He shook as if he were reliving every single nightmare he had ever dreamt.

"'Take it from me,' he cried, his voice sounding shrill as if his throat had been cut. '*I can't bear it anymore!*'

"Then, as he stood and stared into the box, his eyes exploded in their sockets. Flames licked like the tongues of angry serpents from his skull and he roared in pain. My grandfather rushed forward with a long poker, thrusting it like a sword, knocking the box from my father's hands. It clattered to the floor where it landed on its side. Turning his head away and peeking from the corner of his eye, my grandfather forced the lid of the box closed with the poker. He then smothered it as if he were wrestling an untamed animal. He wrapped the chain around the box, passed this through the new lock he had made, and locked it with the key.

"'What have you done?' my grandfather snarled at me, placing the box on the table and covering it with the cloth.

"I rolled onto my back, hands covering my eyes which still smouldered and leaked wispy tendrils of light. 'I'm sorry. I'm sorry,' was all I could murmur. There was banging on the door from outside and I could hear the raised voice of Sir Isake.

"'What's going on in there? Is everything

all right?'

"My grandfather helped me to my feet and guided me toward the stagecoach. He helped me into the carriage and out of sight. 'Stay in there and be quiet!' he barked. I heard him rush back across the workshop to my father. What I didn't know then, but discovered later, was that he wrapped lengths of cloth about my father's eyes like a makeshift bandage.

"'What's going on in there?' Sir Isake demanded from outside.

"'Fletcher's had an accident!' my grandfather shouted back.

"'What sort of an accident? I'm coming in.'

"My grandfather eased my father into the carriage next to me. I heard him bound on top of the stagecoach and take hold of the horse's reins. 'Gee-up!' he roared as Sir Isake threw open the doors. The horses darted forward and galloped out into the city.

"'What's going on?' I heard Sir Isake shout after the stagecoach.

"'The box is repaired for another year!' my grandfather shouted back. 'Can't stop. Fletcher has burnt himself on one of the tools. Got to get him home!'

"'My grandfather ran those horses for three days and nights without rest until we reached the Howling Forests," Abe told Lacey.

"Three of them dropped dead of exhaustion the moment they stopped running."

It was now full dark outside, and the sound of the waves from the Onyx Sea could be heard as they broke along the shoreline. Marco stirred from the corner of the overhang as he continued to rest beneath his cloak.

"So now you know everything," Abe said, his head hung low as if telling his story about what he had done to both himself and his father, weighed like a heavy cloak about his shoulders.

At first Lacey was silent. She wasn't sure what to say. She didn't want to say anything tactless that would only add to the shame and regret that her friend so obviously felt. Lacey took a deep breath and eventually said, "So that's why your father is blind and why you wear those dark glasses."

Abe touched the thick lenses of his spectacles with the tips of his fingers. "When my grandfather calmed down, he made these for me. I wouldn't be able to see otherwise."

Lacey thought for a moment and then added, "You said I know everything – everything about what happened – what you did and why you now feel obliged to go on this journey."

"That's right," Abe replied.

"But you never told me what you saw inside the box. What you saw in the broken piece of mirror."

Abe wrung his hands together, and in a chilling whisper he said, "I saw Draconia."

"What else?" Lacey pushed, desperate to know every detail.

Abe stared at her, his crimson eyes hidden behind the dark lenses. "I saw you in that box, Lacey. I saw *you*!"

Chapter Thirty-Two

Victor lay like a crab, pressed flat on his stomach on the ledge just above the rocky overhang. As Abe finished telling Lacey about how he had snuck into the Splinter and what had happened there, Victor rolled onto his back and grinned up into the moonlight. He hadn't heard the last part of the young man's confession, as he'd dropped his voice to a whisper, but Victor had heard enough.

We'd always known that there had to be a key to the box, but not where to find it! Victor thought to himself, ramming one bony fist into his mouth to smother the sound of his impending laughter.

He remembered how Draconia had worked all of his magic on that lock, but had been unable to open it. In his desperation, and fearing the box might be stolen, he had taken it somewhere safe – somewhere only he could find it once he had found a way of opening the box. Draconia had taken the box to the Grand Station – an ancient railway station that shimmered like a fading star on the other side of the *Emptiness*. Only Draconia possessed enough black magic to cross the *Emptiness* and reach the Grand Station. The only safe way for anyone else wanting to reach it would be to travel on the great *Scorpion Steam* – a train that some said didn't really exist – that such a train was nothing more than myth and legend. Whether such a machine existed it could not be easily reached. It was believed to be buried in a tunnel far below ground, growing old and being eaten away by time and rust. Others spoke of the Scorpion Steam as if it were more than just an age-old steam train – they spoke of it lurking in those dark tunnels below ground waiting for its engine to be stoked and unleashed once more. Victor wasn't sure if such a train existed, but he believed that the Grand Station did. Draconia had been there – that was where he had hidden the box that contained the sliver of mirror that would make him whole once more and fully restore his magic. The Splinter was believed by some to be the epicentre of the Mirror Realm – of all the different worlds and layers, but through his infinite wisdom, Draconia knew better. Draconia knew – believed – that it was the Grand Station that was at the core of the layers and different worlds. It was from that place that all journeys through the layers started and ended. Once it had bustled and heaved with passengers wanting to make journeys through the layers. Although it now stood in ruins and deserted – all journeys from it and through the layers ended – the Grand Station still contained an unimaginable amount of energy and magic. It was this magic and energy that Draconia believed would erode the lock on the box, if not destroy it completely, and set the broken piece of mirror free. But Draconia no longer had to wait for the Grand Station to work its magic. Victor had learnt that it could be opened with a key, but more important than that – he knew where to find it.

The wolf's grandfather who was rotting in Bleakstorm Prison had the key, he grinned to himself. Getting to his feet, Victor crept from the ledge.

When he was far enough away so as not to be heard by Lacey and the others, he muttered under his breath, "I know where to find the key!" He ran along the cliff-edge until he stood high above the rolling black waves of the Onyx Sea. He knew that he must tell Draconia at once. How pleased would he be with his *reflection* when Victor told him this news? Victor hoped that the news of the key would wipe out the mistake he had made by letting Lacey escape him and head once more into the Mirror Realm.

Rubbing his hands together, Victor knelt on the ground at the edge of the cliff-face. Tilting his head back, he gazed into the star-shot sky and flung his arms out. He thought back to his time spent with Araghney, and at once, his heart began to race. Her face swept to the front of his mind, and he pushed it away as he began to rummage through his brain for the spells she had taught him. He hit upon the one that he wanted and then began to chant. *"Beat thy wings from the depths of torment. From the darkness above make thy decent. Raven black and as cold as snow I give you flight Mortality Crow!"*

His waxen lips opened and closed as he whispered the words over and over again until the air all around him filled with the sound of beating. Lowering his gaze, he looked out across the Onyx Sea, and then stepped off the cliff edge. Victor fell down the cliff-face and landed with a thump on something huge and black. The wings of the Mortality Crow he had summoned beat up and down on either side of him as it screeched into the night. Victor wrapped his arms around its sleek, black neck and dug his legs into its sides.

"The Splinter," Victor whispered. *"Take me to the Splinter!"*

The gigantic crow banked to the right as it headed west above the Onyx Sea and toward the Splinter. The night air rushed all around Victor and rippled the bird's glossy black feathers.

"Faster!" Victor roared, digging his heels

deeper into the creature's sides.

The Mortality Crow opened its pointed beak and screeched as it thrust its mighty wings up and down like two giant sails.

Chapter Thirty-Three

While Abe woke Marco, Lacey repacked their supplies and gathered them by the entrance to the overhang. Her mind was still trying to make sense of what her friend, Abe, had told her. She was concerned at how Abe had seen her inside that box. But what had Abe exactly meant by that? Had he seen her reflected back in the shard of mirror that was believed to be inside the box? Perhaps it hadn't been Lacey Abe had seen at all, but her sister, Thea. They were identical twins, after all. Maybe Abe had been mistaken altogether and it had been the Queen he had seen. If the Queen and Thea were reflections of each other, then surely they would look alike. But before Lacey had had the chance to press Abe on the matter, he had jumped to his feet, keen to get going now that the sun had fallen.

As she packed their supplies together, Lacey glanced over at her friends. She could see that Marco was taking small sips of water from the animal skins that Fletcher had filled for them. In the pale milky light of the moon, Lacey could see that Marco looked better than he had earlier, although his skin looked red and blotchy in places where the blisters had been. Even so, Lacey had come to notice that, unlike most people, Marco looked his best – his most jaw-dropping – during nightfall rather than during the day.

Lacey crossed the overhang and looked down at Marco, who sat slumped against the rocky wall. "How are you feeling?" she asked him, handing over some of the uncooked rabbit meat.

Taking the meat from her and tearing it into small chunks, Marco said, "My skin will only heal so many times before it cracks and blisters permanently – or worse. That's the second time I've saved your hide, Lacey. I hope you get to return the favour someday. Then again, perhaps not, huh?"

Lacey looked at his gorgeous face and said, "I'm sorry about what happened to you. I'm sorry that you had to save me again."

Marco made no reply to her apology. He looked away before placing the last of the meat into his mouth. Lacey looked away, too.

She saw Abe standing by the opening to the overhang. "What do we do now?" she asked him.

"We find my grandfather and get the key to that box," Abe said, slinging the supplies over his shoulder.

"You said that the prison is a labyrinth of underground tunnels. Do you have any idea where your grandfather is being held prisoner in that maze?" Lacey asked him.

"Nope," Abe said, bow gripped tight in one claw.

"Do you even know how to get into this prison?"

"Nope," Abe said again, throwing a sling full of inferno berries across his back.

"Well this rescue, or whatever you want to call it, could take forever," Lacey sighed.

"That's why we should get going," Abe said, stepping from beneath the overhang and out onto the shore.

Lacey looked back at Marco, who was now standing in the centre of the cave and straightening his ruffled coat and hooded cloak. Again, Lacey couldn't help but notice how striking he looked, and her heart raced.

"What's got into Abe?" Marco asked her, drawing his sword and inspecting the sharpness of the blade and point.

Lacey shrugged and said, "I'm not sure, but he was telling me how his father lost his sight and..."

"He was telling you about that, was he?" Marco said as if he now understood Abe's disgruntled and sombre mood. "What else did he tell you?" Marco said sheathing his sword.

"That he had seen me..."

But before Lacey had a chance to finish what it was she was about to say, Abe looked back at them and said, "We don't have time to waste. Let's get going."

Lacey and Marco glanced one final time at each other, then made their way from beneath the overhang, joining Abe on the shore.

"See there, in the distance," Abe said, pointing between the cliffs that broke through the sand like jagged skyscrapers. "Can you see those torches burning in the search towers? That's where we're heading."

Lacey and Marco looked at the orange glow that seeped from the towers, illuminating the night sky with halos of light miles away.

"I don't think we will make it by dawn," Marco warned, not wanting to be caught in the glare of the sun again.

"If we hurry we'll be able to reach the prison's perimeter by daybreak. We'll take some shelter during the day, and then we'll break in tomorrow night," Abe said.

Before either one of them had a chance to reply or even put forward another suggestion, Abe had bounded off across the sand and toward a huge valley cut between the cliffs.

Chapter Thirty-Four

As the Mortality Crow swooped toward the Splinter, it opened its mighty talons. Victor buried his head amongst its feathers as it dived for the balcony that jutted from the side of the tower. Fanning its wings on either side, the crow lost altitude and came to rest on the railings that circled the balcony. Wasting no time, Victor slid from the back of the giant bird and climbed over the railings. Flapping his arms out before him, he shooed the crow away. With an ear-splitting squawk, the crow disappeared back into the night in a flurry of silky black feathers.

Victor pushed open the tall glass windows which led from the balcony and hurried into the Queen's chamber.

"Such an unusual entrance, Victor," Draconia rasped from the shadows. "Couldn't you find your mirror?"

On hearing his *reflection's* voice, Victor spun round to find Draconia slumped in his throne on the opposite side of the room to the Queen, who lay lifelessly in her bed.

"Draconia..." Victor began, but was cut short.

"You had better come with good news,

Victor," Draconia gasped, his voice sounding as if he had spent the night chewing on broken glass. "Your carelessness has caused quite a commotion on the other side of the mirrors."

Victor stammered as he tried to find the right words. He was taken aback at how the news of Lacey's escape had reached Draconia.

"Draconia," Victor began, his mouth turning dust-dry, "Lacey was assisted by a Moon Howler and a Blood Runner."

"I don't want excuses, Victor," Draconia hissed.

"And there was this annoying cop…"

"I don't want to hear it, Victor. I'm not interested in hearing about meddling officers of the law. I just want to know how you intend to put right the mess you have caused."

"I do have some important news," Victor began, annoyed that he appeared to be taking the blame for his niece's antics. After all, wasn't it Draconia who was meant to have dealt with Lacey while she had still been in the Mirror Realm? Wasn't it therefore the Guardians' fault that she had escaped back through a mirror? They were the ones that had let her slip back between the layers. But Victor didn't have the stomach, and if he were to be honest, he didn't have the nerve to point this out to Draconia.

"Don't just stand there!" Draconia rasped.

"What is this news?"

"There is a key to the box," Victor said, knowing deep down that he now had the upper hand.

Hearing this, Draconia sat up in his throne. His robes began to flow and rustle all about him.

"What key?" Draconia asked.

"One of the Moon Howlers has it. Before your arrival in the Mirror Realm, two of the Moon Howlers were entrusted to repair the box and fashion a new lock and key for it."

"Find this Moon Howler!" Draconia gasped. "Bring me the key!"

"We already have the Moon Howler and the key," Victor said, a cruel smile of delight playing on his lips. "The Moon Howler is one of the inmates in your prison."

Draconia twitched in his throne on hearing this.

"But we'll have to move with speed. Lacey and her friends are on their way to the prison as we speak, to free the prisoner," Victor warned.

"Impossible," Draconia grinned beneath his hood. "Lacey will never break into that prison, let alone break anyone out."

"Don't be too sure, Draconia," Victor warned with some hesitance. "My niece and her friends, however much it pains me to say it, have proved themselves to be resourceful and sly."

Draconia sat for a moment and listened to the sound of the wind screaming about the top of the tower. "I will destroy the prison and slay everyone within its walls," Draconia whispered more to himself than Victor. "And then we will search through the rubble for this Moon Howler and snatch the key from his lifeless hands."

"But what about Lucia Fay and her pack? She has been a good and loyal governess, as have the rest of the Bitten Hearts," Victor reminded him.

"They can all be replaced," Draconia heaved. "We don't have time for any further delays. If we can find that key, we can open the box. Once the box is open, I will be whole again. The Queen will die, as will her *reflection*. There will be no more of this waiting for the box to erode in the magic radiating from the Grand Station. The Grand Station's power will be all ours, and once more we will be able to open the layers."

Victor began to feel a flutter of excitement in his stomach, as if he had swallowed an angry bee. "I will go to the prison at once..." Victor said, no longer able to wait to be joint ruler of the layers.

"Not you!" Draconia spat. "I need you to go back to the girl, Thea. Lacey's twin sister has been left alone for far too long. After the theatrics that have occurred on the other side of the mirrors, the authorities will soon be after you, and if they find you they *find* her. Go fetch her and bring her into the Mirror Realm."

"But..." Victor stammered, "...I thought you said it would be dangerous... that it could cause complications if Thea and the Queen were brought together... that they could draw strength from one another."

"Don't bring Thea here to the Splinter. Take her far away from here... somewhere..." Draconia thought aloud, "Where there is magic that will prevent them from drawing strength from each other." Then Draconia had it. Why hadn't he thought of it sooner? It was perfect.

"Where should I take her?" Victor asked.

Grinning from beneath his hood, Draconia said, "Take her to Araghney."

"No, not Araghney!" Victor cried. *"Anywhere but Araghney!"*

"Why not?" Draconia asked.

"She has bewitched me," Victor whispered in shame. "I dare not go back there, Draconia... or I fear I may never leave."

"I've asked you to take the girl to her, not *marry her!*" Draconia said. "Pull yourself together, man."

Victor protested. "But..."

297

"No buts, Victor," Draconia shouted over him.

"Araghney," Victor whined, his heart beginning to race again at the very mention of her name.

"Don't fail me again, Victor," Draconia rasped, slumping back into his throne.

Chapter Thirty-Five

The three of them walked all night toward the prison's searchlights. The cliffs towered high above them as they made their way through canyons that had been cut into the hard-packed earth. The sky was cloudless and the moon illuminated their way. Pulling their clothes about them, they shivered against the chill wind that snaked around the cliff-faces.

They had walked in single file for hours, each one lost to their own thoughts. Abe took the lead, bounding ahead then pausing for the others to catch up. Abe knew that if he could return home with his grandfather and nothing else, this may go some way toward gaining him his father's respect and forgiveness.

Marco *blinked* back and forth amongst the rocks. Sometimes he appeared ahead of Lacey, at other times behind her. Marco thought about his family and race of people and how, for him, the mission had to be complete if the curse Draconia had cast upon them were to ever be lifted. Marco conjured pictures of his mother and father in his mind, but their images were somehow distant and foggy as if peering at them through a dirty window. He could just make out his father's long, black hair and firm jawline, and his mother's wistful smile and perfect blue eyes. But that was about it. Everything else was just a blur. The harder Marco tried to picture them, the more their faces turned into those nightmarish *ghosts* that now protected the Howling Forests.

Lacey thought of her sister. Apart from that *freak* of an uncle, Thea was all she had left. She wondered if Thea was still alive and if she shouldn't be with her. But Abe said that Thea could only be saved if the Queen was saved and that had something to do with finding the box. Lacey still hadn't come to terms with losing her parents and she wondered if she ever would, but to lose her twin sister would be unbearable. Casting away the painful thoughts of her parents' deaths, she turned her attention to Abe and his confession.

Lacey was sure that Abe had said the reason she was in the Mirror Realm was because of what he had done. *But how had opening that box brought her into this world?* she wondered, squeezing through a narrow gap in the rocks. With these thoughts at the forefront of her mind, Lacey quickened her step and caught up with her friend.

"You said that everything that had happened was because of what you did," Lacey reminded him.

Abe slowed so Lacey could keep pace with him.

"That's right," Abe said.

"I understand how opening the box caused your father's blindness, but what about everything else? Where do I fit into all of this?"

Marco *blinked* and appeared at Abe's side. Lacey wondered if Marco had done this to offer Abe some moral support or perhaps he, too, wanted to discover the real reason I had been brought into this extraordinary world.

"For hundreds of years, the Mirror Realm has enjoyed a peaceful existence," Abe began to explain. "Like your world, we've had our wars, but like you that was us evolving – learning to appreciate our differences and except one another. But the day I opened the box changed everything, not just for my world but yours, too."

"But this is what I don't understand," Lacey said.

"Within days of me opening the box, a man named Draconia walked out of the wastelands. It is believed that he was attracted to the light that I released. He caught its scent on the wind and followed it like a rabid dog. Shrouded in robes, he strode up to the gates of the Splinter and demanded an audience with the Queen. Compared to him, the Queen's Knights were feeble-minded and they led him high up into the Splinter and into the Queen's chamber."

"It is believed that he held her captive for days at the tip of the Splinter," Marco added, "and during this time she succumbed to his power and she hasn't been seen since. We've heard rumours that she lays asleep and will die when the box is opened and the power that is contained in that shard of mirror is released from the box and absorbed by this stranger – Draconia."

"But she's the Queen," Lacey gasped. "How was she so easily manipulated?"

"No one, not even our Queen, has ever experienced such evil in the Mirror Realm before," Abe said, staring ahead at the towering searchlights. He pulled the collar of his shirt about his neck to block out the cold.

"But where did this stranger – Draconia – come from?" Lacey asked.

"I don't know the answer to that question," Abe said.

Marco *blinked* and reappeared beside her. In doing so his fingertips brushed the back of her hand. Lacey couldn't be sure whether this was a deliberate act or an accident.

"Both Draconia and your uncle want what's inside the box so they can rule both the Mirror Realm and your world," Marco said.

"But how will they achieve such a thing?" Lacey asked in disbelief.

With his unkempt hair billowing out behind him, Abe stared at Lacey from behind his dark glasses. "Some say that Draconia's soul is trapped in that broken piece of mirror. If he should ever open the box and take back that piece of mirror, it will restore his full power and strength. He has managed to destroy much of the Mirror Realm without his full power. Can you imagine what he will be able to achieve?"

"But even if Draconia did open the box, did retrieve this piece of broken mirror and restore his powers, how would he destroy my world?" Lacey frowned. "We have armies..."

"And so did we once," Marco cut in, dismissing her remark. "Your armies will be powerless..."

"But Draconia is just one man..." Lacey fought back.

"He's not a man – not how you think," Abe said, his voice less tempered than Marco's. "Draconia is a witch, sorcerer – *demon*. It is believed that the piece of broken mirror that is hidden in the box came from his mirror that was once smashed. If Draconia gets hold of that missing piece he will be able to reform his mirror and pass through it into your world and take with him his armies, and all the other supernatural creatures like us that have fallen under his spell."

"He'll need a pretty big mirror," Lacey said.

Marco stopped abruptly, taking hold of Lacey's arm. He spun her around to face him. He glared at her and said, "Do you think what we have told you is funny? Do you think this is some kind of game?"

Lacey yanked her arm free of his grip. "No, I don't think this is funny," she seethed, holding her ground. "I just don't understand any of this – just like you didn't understand everything you saw on my side of the mirrors. I'm just trying to make sense of everything you're telling me. You seem to forget that if what you say is true, my sister and I are a part of this mess. My sister is already in great danger. I should be with her, not here with you and having to listen to your bullshit…"

"Okay, okay," Abe said, raising his claws and easing himself between Lacey and Marco. "Let's all just take a deep breath, shall we?"

"Why does he always have to be such a jerk?" Lacey said, folding her arms across her chest, continuing to stare hard at Macro from beneath her hood.

"Because my life depends on you taking this seriously," Marco shot back. "All of our lives depend on you – including your sister's life."

"So you keep saying," Lacey snapped. "But what you're not telling me is why?"

Abe turned his back on Marco and stood directly in front of Lacey so they could no longer stare each other down. Abe took Lacey gently by the shoulders. "Look, if the truth be told, we're not sure why you are so important, but you must be, because I saw you in that mirror – the mirror in the box when I opened it as a boy."

"But how do you know it was me?" Lacey said, her full attention on Abe now that Marco was blocked from her view. "It could have been my sister – we are identical twins. And you said that she was the Queen's reflection or whatever it is you call her."

"It was definitely you, Lacey, that I saw and not your sister," Abe said, over the wind that screamed through the deep canon.

"How can you be so sure?"

"You have a scar – a scar on your left wrist," Abe said.

"How do you know about that? Did you see it when you pulled me by the hand through the mirror?" Then gasping, Lacey added, "Were you spying on me when I was getting undressed in the forest?"

"No," Abe said with a shake of his head and a boyish smile that revealed his jagged teeth.

"Lacey, if I'd been spying on you in the forest as you got undressed, I can assure you it wouldn't have been your wrist that I would have been staring at."

"You're such a jerk, you're no better than Marco," Lacey said, turning away so that Abe couldn't see the half smile that was forming on her lips. She wanted to be mad at Abe as much as she was at Marco, but couldn't be. Lacey believed she knew Abe well enough by now to know that he was a flirt, but nothing more. He was trying to lighten the heavy mood that had fallen over the three of them.

Abe knew that if they were going to be successful in finding the key, and then the box, the three of them would have to get along. They would have to be friends – friends that trusted each other. Abe knew that Marco could be short-tempered and arrogant, but he also suspected that his friend liked Lacey, even if he wouldn't care to admit it. But that was for Marco and Lacey to figure out. For now, Abe, just wanted them to find some common ground.

With her back to both Abe and Marco, Lacey said, "So did you really see that scar on my wrist when you looked into the box?"

"Yes," Abe said. "It was bleeding."

Hearing this, Lacey spun around. "But it has never bled – not that I can remember. It hurts sometimes – but that is all. I can't even remember what caused it. My parents didn't seem to be able to remember either. They said it must have been caused in some minor accident when I was very small – so minor that neither of them could remember such an incident."

"Does it matter how you came by it?" Marco grumbled. "All that matters is that Abe saw it and that's how he knows it was you and not your sister that he saw reflected in that broken piece of mirror."

"Okay, so the scar might not be important, but I think the fact that Abe saw me in that broken piece of mirror – a piece of mirror that you say holds Draconia's power – is pretty significant, don't you think?" Lacey shot back, placing her hands on her hips.

"And that's what we've been trying to tell you all along!" Marco shot back. "At last I think she is finally beginning to wake up and..."

"Piss off," Lacey hissed at him.

"I think what Marco is trying to say," Abe said, trying to diffuse the growing tension again, "is that this is the reason why we believe you are so important in all of this. Why else would you have been reflected in that piece of broken mirror? Some believe that it is you that will be able to open the box..."

"And what then?" Lacey cut in.

"We take the box and the broken piece of mirror to your sister," Marco said, as if Lacey should have already known this.

Lacey scowled at him. "Why take it to her? What's Thea going to do with a broken piece of mirror?"

"We're hoping that she will be able to use the power that is trapped inside it to heal our Queen," Abe said.

"So why not take it straight to the Queen?"

"Because she's being held prisoner by Draconia in the Splinter," Marco sighed as if speaking to a child. "That would not be a great idea, would it – you know, to take the very thing that Draconia wants straight to him."

Although seething inside, Lacey ignored Marco and looked at Abe. Any suggestion of bringing her sister into this mad world was far too serious to allow herself to be drawn into another spat with Marco. "Why do you think my sister will be able to help? She doesn't know anything about this world – the Queen..."

"It's because she is the Queen's reflection, we believe your sister will be able to help her," Abe explained. "And although Marco put it rather bluntly, he is right, it would be too risky to take the box containing the piece of mirror to the Splinter where the Queen is. It will be much safer if we take it through the mirrors and deliver it to your sister. It will be far easier for us to slip into your uncle's house than break into the Splinter."

"But what if my uncle brings Thea into this world, what do we do then?"

Sounding all too confident, Marco took a step closer to Lacey and said, "Draconia wont risk bringing Thea into the Mirror Realm."

"Why not?" Lacey asked.

"Because if brought together, both the Queen and your sister might grow stronger," Abe said. "Draconia wants them both dead, not alive. I think we can safely presume that we will find your sister, Thea, on the other side of the mirrors when we take the box with the mirror to her."

Chapter Thirty-Six

Victor rushed around his kitchen, gathering as many of his potions and remedies that his pockets would hold. He peered out of the kitchen window. Draconia had got him wondering if the police would soon be at his door, and he didn't want to be around when they did. Victor knew that he had to get Thea into the Mirror Realm as soon as possible, but he wanted to take everything that he might need. After all, he didn't know when he would be returning, but when he did, he would be ruler and then the police wouldn't be able to touch him. He'd see to that.

Victor thrust purple, orange, green, and turquoise bottles into his coat and trouser pockets. He rammed spell books and notepads with pages of scribbled handwriting into a small, lizard-skinned satchel. Scooping up the linen cloth which contained the pills he had been force-feeding to Thea, he climbed the stairs two at time and went to her room.

Throwing open the door, he rushed inside. His niece lay on her back, eyes closed and her chest rising up and down at irregular intervals. Victor took one of the pills from the cloth. He opened Thea's mouth and pushed one over her tongue. Holding her jaw shut, he watched for her throat to ripple as the pill forced its way through her body.

Content that Thea had swallowed it, Victor wrapped her in the bedding, gathering her in his arms like a pile of dirty washing. He left the room and carried her downstairs. He glanced around, making sure that he had everything. Facing the fireplace, he closed his eyes and within moments he could see his mirror gleaming in the darkest corner of his mind. He moved toward it, the girl pressed against his chest. Opening his eyes, he grinned at the sight of his mirror standing in the fireplace. With two long strides, Victor carried Thea into the Mirror Realm.

To be continued...

The Mirror Realm
(The Lacey Swift Series)
Book Two
Coming Soon!

More books by Tim O'Rourke

<u>Kiera Hudson Series One</u>

Vampire Shift (Kiera Hudson Series 1) Book 1
Vampire Wake (Kiera Hudson Series 1) Book 2
Vampire Hunt (Kiera Hudson Series 1) Book 3
Vampire Breed (Kiera Hudson Series 1) Book 4
Wolf House (Kiera Hudson Series 1) Book 5
Vampire Hollows (Kiera Hudson Series 1) Book 6

<u>Kiera Hudson Series Two</u>

Dead Flesh (Kiera Hudson Series 2) Book 1
Dead Night (Kiera Hudson Series 2) Book 2
Dead Angels (Kiera Hudson Series 2) Book 3
Dead Statues (Kiera Hudson Series 2) Book 4
Dead Seth (Kiera Hudson Series 2) Book 5
Dead Wolf (Kiera Hudson Series 2) Book 6
Dead Water (Kiera Hudson Series 2) Book 7
Dead Push (Kiera Hudson Series 2) Book 8
Dead Lost (Kiera Hudson Series 2) Book 9

Dead End (Kiera Hudson Series 2) Book 10
Kiera Hudson Series Three
The Creeping Men (Kiera Hudson Series Three) Book 1

The Lethal Infected (Kiera Hudson Series Three) Book 2

The Adoring Artist (Kiera Hudson Series Three) Book 3

The Secret Identity (Kiera Hudson Series Three) Book 4

The White Wolf (Kiera Hudson Series Three) Book 5

The Origins of Cara (Kiera Hudson Series Three) Book 6

The Final Push (Kiera Hudson Series Three) Book 7

The Underground Switch (Kiera Hudson Series Three) Book 8
The Kiera Hudson Prequels
The Kiera Hudson Prequels (Book One)

The Kiera Hudson Prequels (Book Two)
Kiera Hudson & Sammy Carter
Vampire Twin (*Pushed* Trilogy) Book 1

Vampire Chronicle (*Pushed* Trilogy) Book 2
The Alternate World of Kiera Hudson
Wolf Shift
Werewolves of Shade
Werewolves of Shade (Part One)

Werewolves of Shade (Part Two)

Werewolves of Shade (Part Three)
Werewolves of Shade (Part Four)
Werewolves of Shade (Part Five)
Werewolves of Shade (Part Six)
Vampires of Maze
Vampires of Maze (Part One)
Vampires of Maze (Part Two)
Vampires of Maze (Part Three)
Vampires of Maze (Part Four)
Vampires of Maze (Part Five)
Vampires of Maze (Part Six)
Witches of Twisted Den
Witches of Twisted Den (Part One)
Witches of Twisted Den (Part Two)
Witches of Twisted Den (Part Three)
Witches of Twisted Den (Part Four)
Witches of Twisted Den (Part Five)
Witches of Twisted Den (Part Six)
Cowgirl & Creature (Laura Pepper Series)
Cowgirl & Creature (Part One)
Cowgirl & Creature (Part Two)
Cowgirl & Creature (Part Three)
Cowgirl & Creature (Part Four)
Cowgirl & Creature (Part Five)
Cowgirl & Creature (Part Six)
Cowgirl & Creature (Part Seven)
Cowgirl & Creature (Part Eight)
Moon Trilogy
Moonlight (Moon Trilogy) Book 1

Moonbeam (Moon Trilogy) Book 2
Moonshine (Moon Trilogy) Book 3
The Jack Seth Novellas
Hollow Pit (Book One)
Black Hill Farm (Books 1 & 2)
Black Hill Farm (Book 1)
Black Hill Farm: Andy's Diary (Book 2)
Sidney Hart Novels
Witch (A Sidney Hart Novel) Book 1
Yellow (A Sidney Hart Novel) Book 2
The Mirror Realm
The Mirror Realm (Part One)
The Tessa Dark Trilogy
Stilts (Book 1)
Zip (Book 2)
The Mechanic
The Mechanic
The Dark Side of Nightfall Trilogy
The Dark Side of Nightfall (Book One)
The Dark Side of Nightfall (Book Two)
The Dark Side of Nightfall (Book Three)
Samantha Carter Series
Vampire Seeker (Book One)
Vampire Flappers (Book Two)
Vampire Watchmen (Book Three)
Unscathed
Written by Tim O'Rourke & C.J. Pinard

You can contact Tim O'Rourke at
www.facebook.com/timorourkeauthor/ or by
email at kierahudson91@aol.com

12857316R00185

Printed in Great Britain
by Amazon